Fate over Coffee.

By. Mackinsey Mills

For Justin. For showing me how fleeting time truly is. We miss you.

+

For Koda, my sweetest boy.

Part One.

Olivia.

Wren.

The End.

Number 1.

A glimpse into the end.

The sun was setting, it was this dark orange hue almost as if the world around me was on fire. Olivia called me a couple of hours ago to have me meet her in the parking lot of her favorite coffee shop. It's actually our favorite coffee shop. It's such a simplistic little place to sit and have real conversations with people. The lighting is dim and the walls are dark. The mood is set the moment you step inside. I think that's why she loves it so much, she loves a dark aesthetic. I decide to get out of my car and lean up against the hood to smoke a cigarette while I wait. Smoking is my biggest vice, besides her. I haven't had one in months but the feeling rising in my stomach made me feel like it was a good night to enjoy one. It was starting to get chilly out. I went to grab my flannel out the passenger side of my car but then I remembered Liv took it with her this morning. I guess that means I'll be cold until she gets here. I still don't complain when my clothes go missing because she took them, it makes me happy that she wants to wear them. I can tell it gives her comfort when she gets anxious throughout her day. I keep checking the clock that sits on the street outside the coffee shop because she was supposed to be here fifteen minutes ago. It isn't like her to run late without letting me know. The sign on the door of the coffee shop is now lit up in neon, "The Bean" is reflecting off the side of my car. I can't lie, it would be a really cool picture. The kind you want on your wall, you know? A piece of my beautiful car and our favorite coffee shop all creating one unique image. Olivia would really appreciate art that looked like that. She loves different perspectives and sentimental items. I wish she would hurry up and get here so that I can show this to her before the light isn't hitting it right anymore. Plus its getting dark and the snow just melted which means the black ice will probably be bad on the roads tonight and I would rather us not be driving on it if we can help it. I wish there was a way to find out what is taking her so long. I decide to not worry so much and light another one. I check my hair in the side mirrors of the car, it was nice and wavy this morning and I thought it would impress her, even though we have been together for quite a while it's still nice to impress her. My hair has been taken over by the wind and is no longer parted nicely, which blows. I love the way her face lights up every time she sees me. She doesn't even realize she does it half the time because it's a look she gets in her eyes and the way she smiles, it is a natural reaction. Which makes it ten times more attractive to me. To know this girl cares about me that much after all this time. I see headlights brighten over the tiny hill leading up to the coffee shop.

I think Olivia is finally pulling up. Except this car is flying and she doesn't drive like that. I'm tempted to move my car with how fast this person is driving, they are swerving all over the place. The car slides sideways and comes to an abrupt stop, before I could even react to how wild this person just flew in I realized it was Olivia. The car door flung open just as fast as she had been driving. She is terrifying me. I don't like the way this feels. She doesn't ever drive unsafe and doesn't react in a panicking way in public. When she walked around the front of her car it was like watching her move in slow motion, I was studying her to see if she was okay. I immediately knew something was absolutely not okay. Her eyes were dark, blood shot even. She didn't light up when she saw me this time. She had mascara under her eyes and down her cheeks. Her chest was moving up and down faster than I have ever seen, like she was breathing for more than herself. She looked like she was trying to say something to me but the words weren't making it out. I wanted to run to her but it was like my feet were cemented to the ground. Seeing Olivia in that state had me stunned. I don't understand what is happening. As I watch her take slow steps in my direction, she started to walk sideways. Her left shoulder was dropped down like she was distributing weight somewhere else. Maybe she was drinking. I am going to be so fucking mad at her if she drove this intoxicated. My eyes don't leave her as she moves. She is stumbling over her feet, still crying. I need to know what's happening to her.

"Liv, are you okay? What is going on? Have you been drinking?" I started to talk in a panic.

"No. I haven't been drinking Wren. I am so sorry. I'm sorry. I need you to forgive me. Don't hate me, okay? I love you. I love you more than I knew was humanly possible." She was almost screaming these words at me. What is she apologizing for? If she wasn't drinking why is she in this state? I just can't figure out what is happening right in front of me.

"Alright Liv, it's all alright okay. Just come sit with me on the car. Let's get some fresh air and talk about what is going on." I need her to breathe and relax because I can tell as she gets closer to me that she might very well pass out.

"There is nothing left to talk about baby." She is sobbing at this point. My sweet girl looks so broken and I don't know how to help her this time. I haven't ever seen her like this, honestly I have never seen anyone like this before. I went to step forward into her and help her sit down. She needed some water or something. I'm just going to sit her on the curb right here and then go inside the coffee shop and grab her a cup of water, that'll help.

Before I could step into her, she collided into me. I went to move her back and move the hair out of her face but something changed the moment she landed in my arms. She wasn't moving. She went limp. I sat on the ground and held her. She opened her eyes and looked up at me. The relief that came over me was unlike anything I have ever felt.

"Wren, I……"

Number 2.

Wren. Before her and before the end.

Today is going to be a good day. If I speak it into existence it will happen, right? The same old routine of waking up alone, getting ready for work, feeding the dog and leaving for the day to make money at the same place I have been for three years has become something that no longer makes me happy. I used to enjoy the solitude. Not having to answer to anybody, leaving the toilet seat up if I want to, not immediately having to do the dishes, the dog sleeping in bed were all things that brought me the simplest form of happiness. I could simply just be me with no outside debate or ideas. I liked my life that way. Until I woke up a couple of weeks ago next to a girl I had hooked up with the night before and instead of wanting her to grab her things and go, I wanted to make her breakfast. Not because I liked her or felt some weird connection, but because I wanted the conversation. A quiet house no longer seemed like the ideal situation. I wanted someone to talk to about my day, who wanted to know about me and the things I liked to do. I don't think I want anything serious right now, not with just anyone. Maybe just something consistent in my life that isn't my dog.

After my morning thoughts in bed I decide it's time to get ready for work. I need to let Banks out, he's my dog and feed him.

I brushed my teeth and just looked in the mirror for a minute. My hair was awful this morning. It was sticking straight up like I had just hung my head out the window of a moving car. I had bags under my eyes the size of quarters.

I guess that's what I get for staying up late to work on the car in the garage. I needed to pull it together, actually care about my appearance today. I went to the closet and grabbed a white tee shirt and my favorite dark green flannel, ripped jeans and boots. I stepped back into the mirror and was pleasantly surprised. I looked decent today. My outfit did at least. A girl would definitely notice the effort I had put in. I scanned myself up and down starting to judge myself a little too hard. I have a light complexion and dark eyes which gives me a slight upper hand, my smile isn't god awful, but I would definitely like to put on more muscle. Turn myself into the guy I want to be. My mom always told me I needed to love myself in order to properly love another. I am just going to start a journey into self-discovery. Work hard on myself, find a girl and try to give her the world, fix up my car and live a minimalistic life. That's all I want, that's all anyone wants really. I never thought of myself as someone who would want those things at twenty-two. I figured I would be pushing thirty before I wanted to make any big life moves. Times are changing though. It's 1982 in the northern half of Maine, everyone is moving away to the bigger cities, settling down and never looking back. I, on the other hand do not want to go anywhere. I am pretty content with the way life works around here.

I need to work on thinking about all of these big life things and still be productive, I have wasted too much time in my room this morning just staring at the ceiling. I pick myself up, eat some breakfast and head out the door. I started the car and turned up the music as loud as it would go. Jesse's Girl was blaring over the radio and my mood was instantly ten time better. There is something about a good song that just does it for me. It also may make me drive a little too fast, but down this back road it doesn't matter too much. I was fully prepared to have a good day, hell even a good week. It was time to find joy in something new. Maybe I would spend more time in town and meet new people. I could start working on a motorcycle in my free time instead of my car. There are so many things I haven't done because I stayed in this comfortable bubble I call my life for so long. I feel like I have missed so much living for no reason at all. I'm excited to start this new chapter in my life. I have a feeling something really great is going to happen.

I pulled into work and punched in. I did my usually "Hey how are you this morning?" to all my co-workers and went over to my area. I hooked up the small radio, changed out of my nice clothes and into a uniform and immediately went underneath a car. Being a mechanic used to be my dream job. I mean what guy wouldn't want to spend his time getting his hands dirty to restore a car to its original beauty? Well the answer is simple, you go into this job thinking that is exactly what you will be doing. Working on classic cars people only dream of getting their hands on. Boy do I have news for you. Nine times out of ten you are underneath a piece of shit car just trying to get it to run again. It is absolutely not what it's cracked up to be. It has taught me a lot though. My personal vehicle is a pearl black 1969 mustang. Now that is a car. I have a lot of work left to do, but that car is currently everything to me.

The day is dragging by. My hope was that sense I was in such a good mood today that my work day would go by quick and my mood would still be a good one when I went out tonight. Never the less I kept going and watching the time go by.

Finally it's time to clock out. I put back on my nicer clothes and headed back out to my car. I need to decide where I'm going to go this evening. I usually just head home without a second thought but I promised myself I would get out there and do something. I think I'll just run to the local bar and get a drink. It's early enough that it won't be full of people and I might be able to hear myself think. A beer sounds like a good way to end my day. I don't want to hook up with anyone tonight. I just want to be able to say I went out after work and didn't eat another tv dinner.

I sit in my car for a moment. I feel like I needed to take a deep breath for some reason, so I do. I'm beginning to feel a little uneasy. I usually just brush that stuff off and do as I please but tonight feels different. I think the right move here is to just go home. Maybe I am just not ready for this big change like I thought I was. Oh well, I can try again tomorrow.

Number 3.

Olivia. Before him and before the end.

I woke up this morning. A task most people would disregard because we do it every day. For me, this is an accomplishment. I tend to wish I would not open my eyes anymore. Today though, I am grateful. I'm not entirely sure why I feel better today, but I'll take it. It's refreshing to feel this way. I'm usually over thinking this feeling and I find myself scared of it. If I feel this calm and happy something terrible is bound to happen. I'm not the girl who gets to live an exceptional life. I am in fact very ordinary. Which is okay, I guess.

I get out of bed and walk into the bathroom to do my hair. I tend to just throw it up in a bun and go on about my day but today I think I'm going to let my dark curly mane go wild. I'm hoping it'll give me some confidence. I slide into my baggy jeans and put on my favorite off white sweater with the red and navy stripes. I decide to wear my black slip-ons and I throw my books into my bag. I walk downstairs so I can eat something small. I have been running late a lot to work so I would really like to be on time today. I look at the clock above the microwave and realize I am actually making really good time today. I don't have to rush out the door with a bagel hanging out of my mouth. It is an honest to god miracle. Being sad makes it hard to find the motivation to do just about anything productively but today I did my hair and that's a step further than normal. It's the little victories that mean the most to me. I am really proud of myself. I wish I had someone else in my life that was proud of the tiny things that I accomplish in a day that take so much effort. People tend to avoid the introvert. I don't think it's even a thing people do on purpose. It's just because I keep to myself. I don't show interest in going out and being around others so why would they approach me? I have no expectations of people around me anymore. You don't get let down nearly as much that way. Life is much easier when you live it on your own, sadder for sure but easier. I can't even imagine having someone to share my mess with. I am far too complicated and mentally fragile for a normal functioning relationship. I am a lot and I know that. That doesn't stop me from wishing that having all these issues wasn't a deal breaker for someone. I haven't really tried though. I haven't been out on a date in a long time. I was in a relationship for a few years in high school but I'm twenty two this year. I have a lot more to offer than I did back then. I am just afraid. No one shows any interest in me either so I think I have just subconsciously accepted that I won't ever be anyone's first choice.

I check the clock again and it's time for me to head to work. If I get there at a good time I will be able to run across the street and get a coffee. That little coffee shop is my favorite place in town. It's called "The Bean". It has this vibe that just draws you in. Grabbing a large coffee with extra cream and a good book, sitting at the table against the back wall is the best way to clear my head and escape after a long day.

After work today that is exactly what I am going to do. I am going to finish the book I'm currently reading and get a before dinner coffee and relax. That sounds perfect and it gives me something to look forward to. I really am thriving more than usual today. It's nice to find some happiness.

The amount of simple happiness today makes me dread tomorrow. There is just no way I can have two good days in a row. That kind of luck was not written in the stars for me.

Number 4.

Wren.

Its seven o'clock in the morning and it has already been a very long day. I woke up late and the dog got sick in my work boots, then my car wouldn't start. If that hasn't happened to you yet, in the snow, I promise you it will ruin your morning. Not only is it freezing out but you have to sit outside, under the hood of a vehicle trying your best to figure out why on today of all days god has decided that you should have to stand on ice and fix your car.

I finally got it running and I hopped in to speed to work, realizing about ten minutes down the road that I didn't have to go into work today. I took the deepest breath I possibly could and continued driving because there was really no reason to go back home. Plus the sun was coming out which means my favorite coffee shop in town would have its doors wide open for me to smell the beans as I pull up. The smell of fresh coffee is my favorite smell there is.

I made it into town and got out of the car, hoping that if I shut it off it would in fact turn back on when I was finished grabbing my coffee. There was no line which puts a better spin to the morning I've been having.

After ordering I decided to wait outside on the patio for my number to be called. As I was rubbing my hands together trying to get warm, the sun reflected perfectly off the ice covered road and reflected right onto the book store across the street. It had just opened and if I'm being totally honest I had no interest in going in because I don't read much. I don't know why I changed my mind, I don't know if it was the way the light lit up the store almost like I had to go through the doors but I ignored my number being called, I didn't grab my coffee and I started off across the street. As the glare faded and I could see where I was going, I saw her.

I'm not a man who believes in fate. Nor do I believe in love at first sight, but I imagine if I did that this would be the moment I would have decided she was mine and I was going to spend the rest of my life with her. In my own way, I guess I did decide all of those things. Introducing myself would be a good start. My feet couldn't move fast enough, it was like my heart was pulling me faster than I could move. She had already turned around and begun to go back inside the book store. So naturally being my not smooth self I yelled out to her.

"Excuse me miss, hi, yes um..." that's what came out of my mouth. I couldn't believe it. She turned to me so fast I felt like I couldn't catch my breath or my words. Her hair was dark almost like a raven, it shined when the sun hit it. It was curly and beautiful. She was beautiful. Her eyes were so green, but not in that light way most green eyes are. They were more like genuine emeralds. She smiled softly at me and when she went to speak I watched her mouth move but I couldn't hear what she was saying. It was strange, it was as if I didn't need to understand the words leaving her lips. A sense of deja vu almost.

I snapped out of it and heard her repeat to me what she had been saying.

"Is there something I can help you with today?" She said with the smallest giggle like my misunderstanding amused her.

"No I don't think so. I'm not really into books. I just walked over to introduce myself to you." Those words were better but still not great. "I'm Wren. I was grabbing a drink across the street and saw you. You're just so beautiful and..." I realized I was rambling on and decided to stop before it got worse.

"Oh well hello Wren. My name is Olivia. It's a shame you aren't into books seeing as you're speaking to the owner of the book store." She giggled again.

Shit. I blew it. What the hell do I say to her now?

"I mean if you have a book you'd suggest that wouldn't put me to sleep maybe you'd make a reader out of me." That felt better, smoother. Maybe I didn't blow it.

"I have a lot of recommendations, how about I give you two of my favorites on me?" She smiled and ran into her store not waiting for me to answer or follow her. I walked inside to see her rummaging through a huge pile of books behind the counter. She turned to me with a side smile, tucked her hair behind her ear and handed me two books.

"These are the kind of books I continuously re read. I really love the way you can escape in them." She said quietly.

"Thank you, I'll definitely start one of them today. I forgot I didn't have to go into work so I have some time on my hands." I wanted to ask her to go get that coffee I forgot with me but I didn't want to over shoot my shot.

"Thank you for the books." I said abruptly. Followed by "Olivia, would you mind if I came back when I finished both of these books and maybe asked you out for coffee?" Her eyes lit up.

"Yes absolutely. I mean of course I would love to. We could go now if you'd like? I have someone clocking in to work the store right now!" Her excitement was promising. Relieving. I really thought I was going to blow it.

She ran back behind the counter and hung up her apron. She grabbed her things and tied her hair back. I could see more of her features now. Wow. I was mesmerized by her. I could have sworn in that moment I could connect constellations with the freckles that went over her cheeks. She came around the corner and she wrapped his fingers in between mine and said "Are you ready?" That was it.

In that very second a girl I had known for minutes had thrown me into believing in the word fate. There was no way every tiny thing that happened today wasn't meant to bring me into her path. I didn't expect her to take my hand, I didn't expect her to go get coffee with me, I didn't even think she'd give me the time of day. Instead, she gave me something much more important. She made me believe.

A man like me doesn't believe in shit like that. Fate is silly, it's a hopelessly romantic word that makes you believe you are obligated to another person because the stars or god put you together. I work on cars and live alone with a big meaty dog who may look scary but wouldn't hurt a fly. I never had much interest in a relationship. I just did my own thing. Until today. Now that silly, hopelessly romantic word felt like something I wanted. I wanted meeting Olivia to be fate. I wanted it to be written in the stars. What is wrong with me?

Number 6.

Olivia.

The weather is wonderful. I thrive in the cold weather. It brings my soul the sense of peace it needs to stay alive. I got lost in staring out my bedroom window at the blanket of snow and quickly lost track of time. Of course now I'm running late to my own bookstore. You would think when you pull off an incredible thing like opening your own bookstore you would be on time to open the doors every day. I grabbed my clothes off the hanger and threw on my shoes. Running out the door I didn't even pay attention to the ice below my feet and I slid down my steps. Naturally I cried because I cry all the time over the smallest inconvenience, I pulled myself off the ground and headed to my car. Watching every single step I took this time. I tried to remind myself that I was truly feeling okay today and that I just needed to shake off the fall. Maybe today will be different. Maybe today something amazing will happen that will make waking up this morning worth it. Yesterday was good. It was really, truly a good day. I need that to be what happens today too.

I turned the music up as loud as it would go as I drove down the road. I was ready to seize my day. I found this new strength in me that just appeared overnight and I was ready to take advantage of it. Realistically this feeling would last a day or two, maybe only hours so I needed to decide what fearless task I was going to do today.

I am so proud of my bookstore. I named it "A Million Little Lives", I thought it was fitting because when you read a novel you get to escape into a new world, a new life that you create in your mind. I always dreamed of being a writer, I just could never get the words right. So owning a business that might inspire others to write by reading stories really warmed my heart. It was like living through every person who walked through the doors of my store.

I needed to get the new sign out front and the small table of books ready but had a strange feeling I should wait. I tend to get anxious over the simplest of tasks that would take a normal person no more than a single thought to achieve. In the spirit of my new found undeniably temporary strength, I drew on the sign for the day, walked out the doors into the cold and placed it on the sidewalk. I took a deep breath and held my hands together as a way to keep my nerves calm. I did what I needed to do and that was enough. As I turned my back to walk back inside I heard someone start speaking rather loudly in my direction. I stopped and turned back around to see this man standing in-front of me. He was tall, dirty blonde wavy hair, these deep eyes. The kind of man you read about in a novel. He was just stunning. His arms had muscle but not the kind that make you think he worked out too much. Just perfect in every way. I was frozen. I couldn't just stand and stare at him, I needed to open my mouth and speak.

"Is there something I can help you with?" I said with the most awkward smile. He immediately went to answer me.

"No I don't think so. I'm not really into books. I just walked over to introduce myself to you."

I honestly wanted to roll my eyes at him and go on about my day, but something in my gut told me to just keep the conversation alive. Just when I went to tell him my name he started talking again.

"I'm Wren. I was grabbing a drink across the street and saw you. You're just so beautiful." he was rambling and if I'm being truthful it was the most attractive thing about him. The way he lost his words complimenting me. I hated complements. I didn't like myself enough to hear them and say thank you because I just didn't believe them. Never the less I needed to introduce myself to him as well.

"Oh well hello Wren. My name is Olivia. It's a shame you aren't into books seeing as you're speaking to the owner of the book store." I said. I giggled and when it flew from my lips I wanted to pretend it never happened. You can't giggle at a man like that. I shouldn't have even joked with a man like that.

 As I'm sitting here beating myself up over this, we continue our conversation. It was kind of flirty and I kind of loved it. I'm never this comfortable, especially around a guy. I offered to give him some books on the house, hoping again to live vicariously through another person, and maybe even find out if I turned this beautiful man into a reader. When I handed him the books, I could feel my fingers brush against his and I thought I was going to pass out.

He started talking to me, something about thanking me for the books but I was too nervous to even realize that the words were directed at me. I smiled and nodded. Then he kept talking and my ears immediately tuned into him, "Olivia, would you mind if I came back when I finished both of these books and maybe asked you out for coffee?" I felt like me entire body was on fire. I couldn't even hide the amount of happiness that just overcame me. I answered immediately "Yes absolutely. I mean of course I would love to. We could go now if you'd like? I have someone clocking in to work the store right now!" I hoped that my excitement wasn't turning him off of the idea but I hadn't found something to be this happy over in quite a long time.

I didn't realize it at first, but I was running around the counter to grab my stuff. I walked over to him and wrapped my fingers in between his and said "Are you ready?" I couldn't believe how undeniably comfortable I was with him. I was like a different person. Or maybe I was just purely, authentically myself. It was an odd combination of feelings. I was totally in tune with him but also had this feeling of danger. Maybe that's what love feels like. I really wouldn't know one way or the other, but I can't wait to find out.

Number 7.

Wren.

Olivia was a masterpiece. Which is something I would never say about anyone, it's not the way I usually view somebody. When it comes to her the words that pop into my head feel like I'm reading Shakespeare. She brings this raw thing out in the deepest parts of me. I've only known her for less than a day and I never want her to leave. I'm not sure how I feel about it honestly. To feel this way and have only known her for a few hours? I'm going to stop over thinking it and just be present with her. I wasn't sure what I was even going to say after we ordered our coffee, but I didn't have to worry about it because she just started talking and I didn't want her to stop.

"I want to know everything about you" she said in the most upbeat of voices. "Where did you grow up? What's your favorite color? I already know you aren't huge on books. What's your favorite thing to do in your free time? Am I talking too much? It's been a long time sense I've been out with someone I don't know." I couldn't help but laugh at how fast she was talking.

"You're fine I swear. I grew up about an hour north of here in the country part of Maine. My favorite color is blue. In my free time I like to work on my car, she's my baby. And I'm thankful you took a chance on a total stranger." I wanted to ask her all of the same questions but she jumped in so fast.

"You don't feel like a stranger to me though. It's odd. I feel as if I have known you my entire life and then some. Which of course sounds crazy. But not as crazy as referring to your car as your baby." She laughed again, her laugh lit up the entire coffee shop.

"It doesn't sound crazy. For some reason I feel that way too. I'm not the kind of guy to believe in this kind of thing. Not to be too blunt but women come and go. It's not like I set out today looking for anyone, you know? It just happened. It felt like..."

"Fate" she finished my sentence and before I could even acknowledge what she had said to me, she looked stunned and dropped her coffee cup into her lap. I rushed over to her side to help clean her up because she still hasn't snapped out of whatever has her so scared.

"I am so sorry. I can't believe I did that. I just completely blacked out. I'm a mess. Oh please forgive me." She was in a full blown panic. It almost looked like she had seen a ghost. I looked toward the door to see if anyone walked in that could have startled her but there was nobody.

"Olivia, it's okay. You don't have anything to apologize for. Are you burnt? The coffee was still steaming when it fell on you." I said to her softly.

"No I think I'm okay. I feel like such an idiot. This doesn't happen a lot. I just felt my vision go away and I'm just, I'm so sorry" she wouldn't stop apologizing and it hurt to see her this way. I wanted to help her but I didn't know how. She seemed so uneasy, her breathing was all over the place. I didn't want to pry but if I didn't know what was going on I really couldn't do anything for her.

"Liv, what happened?"

I don't know why I called her that but it felt right in the moment. I tried to be as quiet and level as I possibly could. I didn't want her to think I was being pushy but I also needed her to know I was there for her. She looked at me with this sadness that could've broken me.

"I'm okay. Really. It just happens sometimes. I don't want to dive into my problems on a first date. I'm already severely lacking in making a good first impression." I grabbed her hand and said to her "You can tell me anything. I won't judge you or laugh. I won't think you're crazy. I'm here." I needed her to really comprehend the things I was saying to her.

 I could tell she was used to taking on the world alone. She doesn't have to do that anymore. Even if she didn't want to be with me, I'd be there for her. She's that important. Friends, lovers or nothing. I'd hold her hand through the darkness. Don't mistake my want to help her for wanting to save her, because she can do that all on her own. I just want to be the man that stands behind her to watch her rise.

Olivia stood up in front of me, I thought she was going to just walk away. Call it quits before it even started because she was afraid of whatever just came over her. Once again, this woman caught me by surprise. Instead of turning to walk out of the coffee shop, she stepped into my body and kissed me. It blew me away. Time stopped. It really, genuinely stopped moving. I heard nothing around me. Not a single sound wave could have made its way between the two of us. Her lips were warm, like the coffee we were drinking, and oh were they soft. She kissed me so deeply. I didn't know that feeling was possible. Almost as if she was giving me the opportunity to taste pieces of her soul. How is a feeling like this even possible? The words used to describe the way this felt do no justice to the authenticity of her falling into my arms. I soaked every second of this kiss, of her, in. I want to remember each breath she breathed into me for the rest of my life. I am convinced that no other human being on this earth has been given the opportunity to encounter something so other worldly, so incredibly passionate and real. I was overcome not only by Olivia but by this feeling of danger. A feeling like whatever is floating between us right now will be the biggest, most beautiful mistake of my life. I don't may this sensation much mind, because even if this girl costs me everything, I will thank her for the moments before the explosion.

As Olivia backs away from me, I see this light in her eyes. I could tell she had felt every ounce of the same thing that I did.

"Wren, can I say something to you that is going to come off incredibly insane?"

"You say anything you'd like." I said.

"What just happened to me, it was almost as if I had seen a future with you in it flash before my eyes. Until I realized there was no way that it was the future, but the past. I think I have known you, before that is. Like the ocean has always known the tide. Just not in this life. Not as Olivia and Wren. I know this is insane but after kissing you, I felt like before you made any decisions about even wanting to have another coffee with me that you needed to know what I saw. If you don't believe me that's okay, I wouldn't blame you at all" She seemed relieved but also like she was so worried about my response. I can't lie. It was a lot to take in, especially because before this, before meeting Liv, I would think any person who said this to me was insane and needed to be taken to an institution. But I could see it in her and hear it in the way she spoke to me that she wasn't making this up, she believed in what she was saying to me and that in itself was enough for me.

"I believe you. I may not fully understand, but I would like to. Do you want to sit back down and tell me more? Or we could go somewhere else and talk?"

"If you really want to hear about it I think sharing it with you would help calm me down." She said, looking down at her hands. I wanted her to feel comfortable but I could tell that it was going to take much more than words from me for her to be okay around me. So I just lifted my arm up to the side to guide her back towards the table so she could tell me the rest of this story.

Number 8.

Olivia.

I was so nervous to sit across from him again after the events that just unfolded between us. First I have this episode in front of him, followed by going almost catatonic in shock over what just came over me. Wren was really kind to me about the whole thing. It made me feel safe, like he wasn't afraid of my episode so I could be honest with him.

 I stood up and found this wonderfully comfortable courage and fell into him to kiss his lips. It was more than I could ever sanely express, it made me feel like I had totally left my body. I would have given anything for that moment to be frozen in time. To not have to back away from him, to stay completely engulfed in his presence. After our moment was over, I had to tell him what happened to me, the things I saw that made me so uneasy. Trusting him came easy to me. For someone who spends her days overthinking, anxious and afraid of the world around me, being able to be this way with anybody let alone someone like him was a big deal.

"It was this really overwhelming wave of images that came fleeting past my eyes. Almost like a movie was being projected for me to watch except with short snip its and not a full film. I saw you and me, we looked about the same as we do right now. We were dressed differently. You spoke with a British accent, very elegant." I giggled trying to lighten the rest of the story. "I was still just as ordinary. We seemed happy, it looked blissful almost. Totally worry free. As the images of us passed by I could see the love we shared. It was the stuff of fairytales, as if the entire universe collided to create us for one another." I looked up from my hands to catch his eye, to get a sense of what he was thinking. He was just intently listening to me, soaking in my words. So I continued.

"It wouldn't have been a good love story without the heartache though. To really know if you love someone I think you have to be hurt by them. You know? To love them enough to forgive them for being human. As long as the thing that they have done to hurt you doesn't compromise your happiness with them. We all make mistakes, some greater than others, it's the intention inside the mistake that makes the difference. Anyway, I believe our intentions then were simply to give each other the world and in trying to do so we made a catastrophic mess of things. I could see our pain, but it ended abruptly and that is what made me so scared. To have no idea how our story ended, to only feel the pain we caused. Sure, it could be my imagination or the fact that I read and sell books for a living, but it felt real. It worries me. What if the reason we feel so comfortable, the reason that we have fallen into one another's worlds this way, so quickly, is for our fate to be played out as painfully as the past?" I could tell what I was saying was worrying him too. I just couldn't tell if it was because he thought my sanity should be questioned or because he could feel inside himself that what I was saying was true and he didn't know how to process it.

"Could you perhaps say something?" I said to him totally second guessing every move I have made sense I grabbed his hand and walked out of the bookstore.

"Of course, I'm sorry that was just one hell of a thing to hear. I think I believe you. It didn't really feel like a fictional story you just miraculously made up off of the top of your head, but we just met. I'll give you that things between us feel different. I have never experienced anything like this before. You give me a sense of comfort I didn't know I needed. I do need some time to really think about everything you just said. Real or not, I need to decide if it's a risk I want to take. Please don't take that the wrong way. This is just a lot for one afternoon. "

The emotional parts of me wanted to cry because I already felt crazy enough, but he was right. Fate or not this was insane. If he needed to go and not see me again I understood. I didn't want him to go, but I scooped up a tiny amount of bravery and grabbed his hand, looked him in the eyes and took a deep breath.

"Wren, I would never expect you to stay and talk to me after that. The expectation after a conversation like that is you run off and tell your friends you met this crazy chick at a bookstore today and wished you had gotten coffee alone. All of that is okay, too. I just felt like no matter what you thought of today and what I had to say, for some reason, you needed to know."

"I don't think you're crazy, darling." He said softly.

Darling is a word I had no idea I could love so much.

"I think, for today anyway, parting ways is the best idea. The space between us may help both of us decide if this entire encounter could even be considered normal." I said, trying my best to hold my ground.

"Okay, yeah. I think that's the best idea." He looked disappointed and I hated not knowing why.

"Alright well, I'm going to go back to my store, thank you for the coffee and for the conversation." I said, rushing to grab my things because I could just feel tears welling in my eyes. I can be extremely over emotional, ninety percent of the time.

I walked away from him, not knowing if he'd ever walk back through the doors of my store again. I wouldn't blame him if he didn't. Today was a lot. I don't even know how to feel about it. I decided to push this overwhelming encounter with Wren out of my head and go spend the rest of my day comforted and totally surrounded by my books. That is my favorite way to calm down. I like the idea of going to a lake or the woods and breathing in the silence, but my mind is far too paranoid for that to happen.

I smiled and briefly talked to one of my employees. Her name is Aria. She is so sweet and helpful and literally the perfect person to be working with today. She would ask why I seem off but wouldn't pry if I wasn't up to talking. I needed a real distraction. Telling myself to keep him out of my head was a task in its own. How do I not think about the insanely attractive man who walked across the street, into my store to introduce himself to me. Someone who was strong, bruiting but emotionally open to me? I had just met him and he suddenly became the center of my day. I couldn't stop myself from picturing the intense way we kissed. I caught myself biting my lip thinking about it. I was living in a book, I am convinced. There is no way the events that unfolded today were a real life scenario that happened to me. It's just impossible. No matter how impossible it felt, the day dreaming would not cease. He was such a captivating person. Not in a way that all girl would swoon at the sight of him. More so in a way that he spoke to me like I was a piece of paper standing in front of him waiting for him to spill his poetry onto me. He was undeniably handsome, he was kind. The combination any woman on the planet would kill for. I started to think walking away from him was a mistake. I slowly begun to not care how crazy I sounded when I told him what I had seen. I wanted to be with him. In the presence of him. Wren was intoxicating and my high would not burn out, I remained on fire.

I ran to the store window to see if he was still across the street. I couldn't see into the coffee shop, but from him referring to his car as his baby, I assumed that beautiful black car sitting in front of the shop was his. I had a decision to make. To run to him and hope he is thinking the same things as I am. Or to stay inside my store and hope he comes back in one day.

It took me a solid fifteen minutes to get anywhere close to a decision because I over thought the over thinking. I think I'm just going to go for it. I either lose it all or gain everything. With the story I told him at the coffee shop, I think I may be closer to losing it all. I needed to take this leap for myself. I looked down at my feet and started forcing myself toward my front door. Repeating to myself over and over again that I could do this. I could turn the knob and walk across the street. I could look him in the eyes again. I had to do it, I owed it to fate, right? I started over thinking again. What if what I saw is real? What if the story of Olivia and Wren is one that ends terribly? Oh but what if it's beautiful.

"Damn it Olivia just fucking go for it." I said to myself in the sternest internal voice I could come up with.

Here goes everything. My hand reached for the door knob and a shadow cast itself over my arms. I looked up and he was standing on the other side of the door looking at me. Was he contemplating the same thing? Do we open this door and see what happens? Or do we keep this thin layer of glass between us and never know? I didn't even have moment to think before my heart took over and I turned the knob. I opened the door to face him, more nervous than when he first came over to me to say hello. I could hear his breathing getting deeper. I lifted my hand to his cheek. His face was hot, the way mine gets when I'm anxious.

"I know we said we should part ways and figure out how today made us feel, but I couldn't stop thinking about you. Only an hour had gone by and all I wanted to do was hear you talk. I think whatever is between us is real and people are going to judge us, they are going to think that we are insane. That we should be locked away in strait jackets together, but honestly Olivia I just don't care." He said to me.

"I agree. I don't care either. This is either going to be the most wonderful thing we ever do, or it'll completely shatter us into something we can never put back together. With that being said, I need to know that the next few things I say to you are okay. I won't let you go into this blindly." I said, worried this was about to be a deal breaker and create a broken moment. "I have so many problems you honestly wouldn't believe me if I told them all to you. I'm really sad all the time and maybe being around you will change that but my moods are never guaranteed but I will try my best if you are willing to give me a chance."

"Do you honestly think that after the things that were said over coffee that you having problems just like every other human being is going to be a problem for me? Darling, we all have baggage. I'm a hot head. I get angry easy and struggle with my ego. Before meeting you today I probably would have tried to hook up with your employee over there and never call her again. I drink a lot and I cuss too much, but I will work on all of it for you. If you accept me as I am, too. "He said, he came off so hopeful. It was amazing how quickly he made me believe that there could really be something between us that wouldn't end in complete and utter disaster.

"I think I can deal with that." I said to him.

"Then it's settled. We will spend our days exploring what we could have and seeing where it takes us." Wren smiled so big.

"Would you like to start now?" I smiled but down at my hands, nervous for the response. I'm never that blunt with someone, but with him I feel like I can just say what's on my mind with zero consequence.

"I would really like that. Unfortunately I have to go. I have to let my dog out and work on the car some today."

"What if I bring you a beer and dinner tonight while you work on your car?" I offered.

"You would really want to do that?" He seemed so surprised by the gesture.

"I wouldn't mind at all. I think it would be cool to see you work on your car. Plus I'm a great cook. When it comes to instant food." I laughed, trying to make him smile.

"That sounds perfect. Do you have a piece of paper I can write my address on for you?"

"Yes I do, just give me one minute." I was looking forward to tonight. To see him do the thing he loves to do, he can judge my mediocre cooking and we can drink. I handed him the paper and a pen so he could give me his address.

I wanted to kiss him more than anything. I knew I needed to wait. I would seem him later tonight and we would be alone. At his house. I suddenly went from excited to nervous. What if he is expecting more from me than dinner? Do I want to do that with him already? We did throw around the word fate over coffee. So I guess it wouldn't be that big of a deal in comparison. I walked him out of my store still thinking about how tonight would go when we were alone. He kissed me on the cheek and made me blush. He went to get in his car and said
"I will see you tonight darling." I smiled the biggest smile and waved goodbye. My mind started racing with the scenarios that could unfold after dinner tonight. He could either decide in that time that things happened way too fast and that this was indeed way too insane for us to continue, or things move forward on the path we have already started down and I end up in bed with him. The more I think about it, the more I want him. How could I want all of this with a man who is really a total stranger, whether he feels like one or not. I need to continue to be unguarded and let this whirlwind continue to blow.

All of this was kind of amazing. I felt like I was living in my very own book. A story written just for us to live out. I wanted to skim the pages and get a glimpse into what is going to happen next but where is the adventure in that? I took a few deep breaths and told myself "Liv, you deserve this. This unrealistic love story you have craved sense you were a little girl. Go live it." I was right. I needed to go live it. This was a once in a lifetime thing that just unfolded right in front of me. I have never been so glad that I got out of bed in the morning.

I walked over to the front desk to ask Aria if she would be okay with closing tonight so I could leave soon to go get dressed and attempt to cook for him. I needed to run by the store too because I promised him beer. Thankfully, Aria overheard the entire thing and was more than happy to close for me. Her exact words were "Olivia if you don't get out of this dusty book store right now and go get done up for that man, I'm going to go in your place." She couldn't stop smiling at me, I knew she had eavesdropped but I didn't realize that when she said she overheard she meant the entire, word for word event. It almost made me happy that she listened in because truthfully I don't have anyone to talk to about it. She may be my employee but she's the closest thing I have to a friend. I started gathering my things while she went on and on about how gorgeous he was and how she just couldn't believe we'd never seen him before. She was right, I don't understand how in a town this size that we have never seen him around. He is extremely hard to miss. I don't go out a lot but I have gone to the bar down the road a few times with Aria even before I hired her and I definitely have not seen him before.

I started off to my car. I was ready to run this errand and go pick out an outfit that would impress him. I'm not entirely sure why I wanted to try so hard, after all he thought I was beautiful with my messy curls, no makeup, an apron and holding old books. Now that I'm thinking about it, how the fuck did Wren find me attractive, let alone call me beautiful. Whatever his reasons are, I'm thankful for him.

Even if this goes nowhere and we had this intense twenty four hours, I will be thankful.

The store trip is taking longer than I wanted because I forgot to ask what kind of beer he liked. How am I supposed to guess what kind of beer he would want for dinner? Come to think of it, I don't know what he would like for dinner either. I'm just going to hope for the best. I grabbed a generic beer that most people like and decided to make him Italian for dinner because I can cook noodles. I go to check out and I'm still making pretty good time. I thanked the lady at the counter and walked out of the store.

When I pull in the driveway I grabbed my grocery bags and ran into the house. I put everything in the fridge and head straight up to my room to find something to wear. I look in the mirror at myself and realized my outfit was kind of nice. It's my favorite sweater which will keep me comfortable with myself, maybe if I just change into nicer pants and put on some makeup I will feel better and just feel like me. I put on some mascara that made my dark green eyes pop significantly. I put on some blush and a light shade of lipstick and stepped back to look at my face in the bathroom mirror. I was really taken back. I haven't really appreciated my features before. I didn't pay them much mind, but he made me want to. I wanted to see what he saw. I was pretty happy with the way I looked for our little at home date tonight so I went down to the kitchen to start cooking him dinner.

I kept thinking about all the possibilities. This night has the potential to be everything I ever wanted. It also has the potential to be an absolute fucking disaster. I chose to keep things positive and daydream about how amazing it will be to kiss him again.

His lips felt like silk. They were warm and soft. I could have just inhaled him forever. He put his hand on the base of my back and pulled me into him. It felt like a title wave flew through my entire body. He kissed me just as deep as I kissed him. It was this reciprocated, lustful pull into one another. I could feel that same desire pulsing through him just as it did me. I wanted more of him. I put my hands on my thighs and made the adult decision to stop daydreaming and actually work on this dinner so I can go see him. Being present with him will be much better than sitting here picturing a kiss.

I checked the water in the pot, it was finally boiling so I dropped the noodles in the pot and started making the rest of the food. I made him a cesar salad to go with it, hoping if I made it look fancy he would be impressed with the dinner I'm brining.

Dinner is done. I'm dressed and ready to go. Then the overwhelming nerves hit me like a truck. I was so distracted by cooking that I forgot I was actually driving over to his house to have dinner. I needed to get my shit together. The last thing I need to do is overthink myself into a panic and end up late. I don't want to make him upset. Especially after the shit I pulled today. I put all the food in containers and put all the containers in a bag, walked out the door and got into my car. I looked at his address and was pleasantly surprised to see he didn't live that far from me. It was also strange to think he lived that close to me and we have never crossed paths. The world is weird that way. I put the car in drive and said to myself, "Here goes nothing."

Number 9.

Wren.

I got so caught up in working on my car I lost track of time. I only popped my head up because Banks started barking for dinner. "Shit." I thought to myself, Olivia is going to be here soon and I am disgusting. I didn't clean the house up and I have grease on my face. I think I'm going to rush and get a shower before she gets here. I know she probably wouldn't care that I look like this but I do. I fed the dog and hopped in the shower. I rinsed off and thought about kissing her. It made my heart pound. I can't wait to see her again. I stepped out and dried off, threw on a tee shirt and jeans, hoping that she would appreciate my simplicity tonight. I made my hair look decent and towel dried it. I was about to give myself a pep talk to calm my nerves and then headlights lit up my side wall. I looked out the window to see who it was, and it's her, she's here. I almost tripped down the stairs trying to slide my shoes on and get to the door so I could help her carry what she brought inside.

I opened the door and her eyes met mine. I couldn't help but smile. She is just so beautiful, still in the same sweater from today. I loved that, she is so authentic. She walked up to me and said "I hope you like Italian. I should have asked you what you wanted to eat but it slipped my mind and I just assumed that everyone likes Italian. I hope you like it."

"Italian sounds perfect. Thank you for cooking. I'm not picky. You could have made us a grilled cheese to split and I would have been happy." I said. She laughed and seemed relieved.

"I wanted to make you something better than that, but I will remember the grilled cheese idea for next time." She was getting more comfortable, at least it seemed like she was.

"I'll hold you to that." I said as I opened the door up for her.

I forgot to light the candles that I set out. I led her into the dining room and told her sense she cooked it serve. I ran to get the matches so I could light the candles and poured her a glass of wine that I had left over. I put the food on to my only glass plates and served her pasta and wine. I liked seeing her like this. She didn't seem anxious or like she was thinking about the coffee shop earlier.

"So, now it's your turn to tell me something about yourself. You already asked me questions earlier so now you get to enlighten me on who Olivia is." I said hoping she would open up to me a little bit.

"Okay well, my favorite color is green. I have lived here my whole life and I love owning my own book store. My favorite thing to do is go to Beans and read with a huge cup of coffee. I crave a life different than what I have. Oh and I think you're pretty amazing." She was so quiet when she said she thought I was amazing, she even tucked her hair behind her ear. I could watch her tell me about herself all night. I hope that's all she wants to do. I want to know every single detail about her and about her life.

"I think you're pretty amazing, too." I said to her. "I love that you love coffee houses and books. I can see how passionate you are about it. I could see myself enjoying books if you were the one reading them to me." I was hoping when I said that she would blush. Her cheeks are naturally kind of flushed so I'm not sure I could tell the difference.

"Is that so?" She said putting her hand on her face.

"Yeah, I really think I could get into books if a girl like you read them to me."

"I can do that for you. Did you bring in the books I sent home with you today?" she asked.

"I did! They are up in my room on the nightstand, after we eat maybe we can start one together." I hoped she wouldn't feel like I was just trying to get her up to my room. I didn't want her to feel uncomfortable. I could easily walk her into my room to get those books and not even kiss her. For the simple fact that I would never want her to feel like that's all I wanted from her. I wanted so much more than something physical with her. If what was said between us at the coffee shop showed me anything, it was that no matter how insane this is, no matter how unbelievable and unrealistic our story started, I wanted more than anything to see how it ends. I didn't care about the way she all but blacked out, I didn't care about her troubled past, and all I wanted to do was know her.

"You could give me a tour of the house and I could meet your dog, I could give him tons of love and then you could show me your room and maybe grab a book?" when she said that, I couldn't tell if she was flirting with me and actually wanted to go to my room or if she was being polite.

"That sounds like a plan." I said with my mouth half full. Her cooking was really good. I was impressed. It's better than what I can cook that's for sure.

"I feel like I need to apologize to you. Today was not exactly ideal as far as meeting you for the first time goes. I don't really understand what happened. I just don't want you to base your opinion of me off of the coffee shop. I'm not exactly impressive but I promise you I am not the girl who just throws the word fate around and blacks out randomly. I genuinely sound like a psychopath."

"I don't think you are crazy. I was kind of overcome with feelings for you too. That doesn't happen to me either. I wish you would stop apologizing for earlier. Even if I actually did think you were insane, we are still here having dinner and we can restart from here, okay?" I wanted her to relax some. I didn't want her dwelling on earlier. I wanted to just worry about right now. Enjoy the time and the conversation. I think I am going to kiss her again. That will lighten things up and hopefully distract her.

I stood up and walked over to her. I pulled her chair off to the side and grabbed both of her hands. She was in front of me now, I stared into her eyes and brushed her hair away from her face. If I didn't crave her lips so badly, I could have just stared into her eyes. Being this close to her I can see all of the tiny gold flecks in the green. I have never seen eyes like that, the kind I can get lost in. I put my hand on her cheek and let the other hand rest on her back, I let her naturally fall into me and I kissed her. It was better than the first kiss, which I did not think was possible. This time, it took my breath away and I couldn't get it back. I didn't want to breathe again if it meant her stepping out of my kiss. Her breathing shifted and she sighed. Hearing Olivia sigh was like listening to your favorite song. In that moment, I wanted her. More than conversation, more than this kiss, I wanted to be completely wrapped up in her. I wanted to hear her sigh but louder. I hated myself for how bad I wanted her. I am just going to follow her lead. I can't rush things with her, I don't want to risk it. She pulled back for a moment.

"Wren." Her breathing was so heavy. "Show me your bedroom."

I picked her up from underneath her thighs, I directed her legs around my waist and carried her up the stairs. She kept her body pressed against me, leaving no space between us. I nudged my bedroom door open and walked over to the bed. I laid her down and stood there, staring at this stunning creature laying on my bed sheets. Seeing her there like that gave me that same feeling that rushed over me earlier, the only thing that popped into my head was the word fate. This girl was always meant to be here with me. As I made the decision to lay on top of her and soak her in some more, she watched each move I made. It made me nervous. I've never been nervous in bed with a girl before, ever. She made me feel every emotion I didn't believe in.

Number 10.

Olivia.

I came here tonight with every intention to just be in his company, get to know him and have pleasant conversation. Instead, we had talked in the simplest of ways, I shared some of my anxious thoughts and we ended up here. I am in Wren's bed, staring up at him. I have spent this entire day feeling this undeniable sense of pure comfort with this man, but in this moment I am just nervous. I don't have nearly enough confidence for him to see me naked. Wren is perfect in every way. I will never compare to the women he has been with before. I am doing my very best to just take in being with him this way and to not continuously over think, but it's becoming more and more difficult to not be scared when he is kissing me this way. It is passionate and honest, his intentions are clear. Those intentions however, are not just lust filled. I can tell he just wants to be with me, he cares. Which is an odd feeling to feel from a man I have known for a single day. I'm not complaining, I am honored to be cared for by him.

I had this thought rush through my head as he laid his body on top of me, that I should just give in to my desires for once and not be afraid. I deserved this, to be entangled in this man. I could feel his heartbeat pounding through his chest onto mine. We were pressed against one another in such a way it almost felt as if our breathing became in sync. He removed his lips from mine and placed them on my neck. I could feel my back begin to arch and I let out a sigh. The feeling of his mouth, his breath on my body was unlike anything I have ever experienced before. I haven't been with many men but I know for a fact it isn't normal to feel what I'm feeling. This is something that could only be felt with Wren.

"Wren, do you want me?" I was surprised this thought was turned into words and said out loud. He looked at me and had this smirk roll across his face.

"It would be an honor to devour you, Olivia." He said into my ear.

There aren't even words to describe the way that this man just became utterly in charge of my body with those words. If he wanted to devour me, I was going to let him. There was no over thinking at this point, there was no more trying to deny how badly I wanted him. Once he said that to me, my body gave into him. I felt myself go almost limp in pure relaxation and I just melted into him.

His hands slid up my arms as he moved them above my head. He grabbed my shirt and slid it off of me. I ran my hands underneath his shirt and lifted his off of him as well. I laid back down and felt his fingers fumble with the buttons on my pants. I heard the zipper move down and my heart started pounding. He pulled my pants off of my legs and stood up in front of me. As he threw my pants down onto his floor, he took his off too. All that was left between us was a bra and both of our underwear. He went to get back on top of me and before he could I just ripped my bra off of my body along with my underwear, wrapped my hands around his back and pulled him on top of me. Don't get me wrong, all of these intimate moments leading us here were like magic, but I wanted him and I wanted him now.

His face sat in front of mine, our noses were touching and our mouths were open but our lips hadn't met again quite yet.

"Is this what you want?" he asked kindly.

"Yes." I could barely get that word out of my mouth as he entered my body.

The way our bodies moved together was kind of beautiful. It was almost as if I didn't have to think about what I was doing, I just knew already. Almost as if this wasn't the first time we did this. Which makes sense after what I saw earlier. I didn't want to think about that right now. I just wanted to enjoy this.

Wren let out this moan that shook every single nerve in my body. I didn't want him to stop, the sounds he was making couldn't be describe with any amount of words, no novelist could write the way he expressed his pleasure. I didn't realize it but I was moaning right back.

I now know why the stars make us less afraid of the night. It can be pitch black in the world around us and one single star can light up a path toward your home. I found that in him. I am home wrapped up in him.

As we finished and he rolled over next to me, I nuzzled into his chest. We didn't say a word. We shared the silence. I could feel myself drifting off to sleep. I had never been okay with staying over at someone's house after sleeping together, but just like everything else that pertained to him, it felt right. He began to run his fingers through my hair.

"You can sleep my darling. I will be here when you wake up." He said sweetly.

I allowed myself to sink into the bed and drift off.

Only moments after falling asleep I had started to dream. It was of those fleeting images I had seen before me in the coffee shop. I was able to really see those two people that reminded me so much of Wren and I. They truly were very happy. She was beautiful, young and so vibrant. She had brown, thick hair and dark eyes. She smiled as if everything in her world was as it should be. They were both dressed in clothes much older than the times now. I saw a newspaper sitting on a table that they stood near, the year read 1932. I hoped I wouldn't wake any time soon and I could see more of how their story unfolded. The man that reminded me of Wren was tall, he had this light brown almost ginger like hair. His eyes were light and when he looked at her it was like she was his queen and he would protect her at all costs. They ran around this sweet little town and all they did was laugh, it was incredible to watch two people so deeply in love with one another. Like a flash of lightening, the tone of the dream changed. It got dark, it was no longer this loving dream of two people who were madly in love. It became sad, the kind of sad that strikes you right in the chest and makes you ache. I couldn't see either of them anymore. All I could see was rolling rain clouds and darkness. I started to hear something, though. It sounded like screaming. The woman who I believed in my soul was at one point I was, was screaming in an immense amount of pain. Not a physical pain like she had been hurt, but the kind of pain you let out in loud bursts when you have lost someone. In between her moments of pain I heard another voice, it was his voice. It was quiet and very faint. It was almost too quiet to make out completely. If I heard him right he was just begging her to calm down, for her to breathe. Then the clouds begun to part and there were clear images again. I felt like there was something that I needed to be shown. I could see both of their figures start to appear. She was pacing back and forth, hyperventilating. He was laying on the ground clutching his chest. I am unsure what happened in between the things I have been able to see, but I could feel it in her that she knew she was about to lose him. I saw a gun sitting next to his body. I watched her find it with her eyes. She picked it up and kneeled next to him. I had begun to wonder who would have shot him right in front of her eyes. Maybe they had been mugged. Maybe he had enemies that wouldn't care if another person was present to witness the crime be committed. Either way, their time was up and I knew it. I could see that she was not going to live without him. I wanted to yell to her, to tell her not to do it but the words wouldn't make it to there in time. She kissed him and said "I will be with you always my love." And she pulled the gun on herself. The sound of the shot ringing startled me awake. I was grateful to be woken by this. I couldn't handle seeing anymore. I had no desire to know their names or to know if in truth, these people used to be us. This dream broke something inside of me. All I could hope was that I never had to see it again.

Wren was still sound asleep next to me. I let myself weep for the couple I just saw die in my mind and curled back up next to him. I breathed him in and fell back into a deep sleep.

Number 11.

Wren.

The sun beaming directly into my eyes is what woke me up. I rolled over and saw Olivia sleeping so peacefully. She was so beautiful. Her curls fell in her face while she slept so you could only see tiny details of her face, a few freckles, the creases of her eyes and the tip of her nose. I wanted to just let her sleep so I think the right move would be to quietly get up and make her breakfast. I leaned over to kiss her on the forehead and slid out of bed. Hopefully she will rest for a while and I can make up for the lack of conversation last night. Maybe if she doesn't have to work today sense it's a Saturday, I can take her into town. We really do live in such a beautiful area of Maine. There is this street in town where "The Bean" coffee shop is and her book store that is about a mile and half long full of restaurants and stores. At night all the trees along the sidewalk are lit up. On most Friday nights there are live bands playing at the bar that you can hear while you're walking. If you turn right after Olivia's book store you can head straight down to the water. It's usually pretty cold here but the view is still breathtaking. Even with living here for long, nothing beats seeing the sunset over the water and walking into town to eat or go to the bar on the weekends. It's like a getaway from life that's always there. It's homey here. I think it would be nice to experience all of those things with her instead of on my own. I don't want to push it though, I mean within a day we have already slept together and through around the word fate. Coming on too strong may have gone out the window but I still don't want to scare her off. There isn't any harm in asking her. The worst she can say is no.

I think I'm going to make her blueberry muffins and coffee for breakfast. When we were out yesterday ordering our coffee I noticed her eyeing the muffins. Hopefully she thinks that my noticing was romantic and not strange. At the very least the smell of freshly brewed coffee and muffins in the morning are a great thing to wake up to.

I find myself wondering if last night was too much. My only intentions going into dinner were to really get a chance to get to know her, to have a nice conversation, kiss her and enjoy her company. That idea changed so rapidly, I don't want that to have jeopardized an already shaky relationship. I could tell her feelings were reciprocated and in the moment that helped.

I got lost in my thoughts and realized I was about to burn the muffins. I pulled them out of the oven and set them on the stove. Banks came running up under my feet so I let him outside for a few minutes and fed him. I was looking forward to Olivia meeting him. He is basically my best friend and she seemed interested in loving on him last night. I walked out with Banks to pick some flowers from the back garden my mom had planted. Fresh flowers, coffee and food to wake up to sounds like something that would make her happy. I should have grabbed the books off the nightstand to add to the table this morning too.

I went back inside with Banks and started setting the table up and removing our dinner plates from last night. I am honestly surprised that Banks didn't jump up and eat everything that was left out. I put all the left overs in the fridge, the ones I could salvage anyway and poured some coffee. My coffee is nowhere near as good as the stuff in town but it'll get you moving. I am anxious for Liv to wake up. I know she needs to rest but I also really want to ask her to spend the day with me. I would even be willing to help her at the store if that meant getting to know her better.

Reading truly isn't my thing but for her I would try my very best to make it into something I can at least pretend to enjoy. I can hear the floor board's creek above my head. She is up and moving. I jumped up to put the flowers in water so the table looked nice when she made it down stairs. My heart started pounding. I am almost beginning to hate how nervous this girl makes me.

As she made it to the bottom of the steps I came out of the dining room to meet her. She was wearing my shirt from last night, her underwear and socks. Her curls were sticking out everywhere and her eyes still looked tired. I am not totally sure if it was in my head or not but I think my mouth fell open at the sight of her. She looked beautiful when I first saw her and when she showed up to my house last night, every inch of her just blew me away. There is just something different about her right now. It's bigger then the word beautiful. That's almost an insulting way to describe the way she looks right now. I can't take my eyes off of her. She has this smirk on her face and she did her hair tuck thing again.

"Good morning Wren. How did you sleep?" She said to me in the sleepiest tone of voice.

"I slept like a rock. How did you sleep?"

"I had a nightmare but after that I slept great. The bed was soft and you kept me warm." She was blushing. I loved how red her cheeks got.

"I'm sorry you had a nightmare, you should have woken me up. I would have stayed up with you until you were ready to go back to sleep." I said.

"Oh no, I wasn't going to wake you up over something silly like that. Your house smells lovely. I can smell the coffee but I can't make out what else is in the air."

"I made you breakfast." I lifted my arm up to gesture her inside the dining room. She had her arms tangled together sitting at her chest and she walked almost on her tip toes into the dining room. Her face lit up. I was so glad she was happy with everything I did. Impressing her has officially become my favorite thing to do.

We sat across from each other and ate. It was so casual this morning. The conversation was easy and comfortable. As if we really had known each other our whole lives. The sun came in through window just right and made her hair shimmer and her eyes light up, it really highlighted the brown flecks inside her green. I have never seen another human being crafted like this, almost ethereal. She deserves to be painted. To be admired as art.

"Thank you for breakfast. And for letting me stay over last night." Olivia said.

"Yeah of course, any time." I really meant it, any time. "I was wondering, if you don't have to go into the store today if you'd like to spend the day with me?" I asked.

"I have to go in for an hour this morning to open and make sure everything was finished up last night. After that though I would love to spend the day with you." She said smiling.

"Really? That's amazing. Okay, so I can come pick you up at the store and we can just go off for the day. I can drive you there too if you want me to." I said in the hopes that she would take that offer and she would have to come get her car from my house later in the evening.

"Yes, I would love that. Could we leave soon so I can run by my house to get a change of clothes and shower before I go into the store?"

"Of course. While you finishing eating I will go get dressed and send Banks in here to keep you company." I said as I walked over to the gate to let Banks back in. Her eyes lit up when she saw him run in toward her.

"Oh why hello you sweet furry beast. How are you this morning? Did you sleep well?" Watching her talk to my dog like he was her favorite thing in the world was cool to see. His tail was wagging and he kept kissing her face.

"Now that the two of you are acquainted I am going to rinse off in the shower and throw on some clothes. I will be back down shortly."

"No rush, I have the best company there is." She replied while she was rubbing Banks' belly.

I jump in the shower and just rinse off so I don't have bed head on our date today. I am just going to wear the same thing I always wear, a white tee shirt. I want to look nice but also don't want to seem like I'm trying too hard so instead of a flannel this time I go with a jean jacket. I hop out of the shower, towel dry my hair and throw on my best pair of plaid pants. When I walk out of the bathroom, she is in my room changing back into her clothes from the night before. I lean against the door opening and just watch, arms crossed with a smile on my face. She looks up at me and laughed.

"What are you looking at?" she said mid laugh.

"Just admiring my view is all." I answered.

I could tell that answer made her happy because she didn't ask me to look away. I could get used to this. She finished getting dressed and then we both walked out the front door ready to start the day together.

"Just give me the directions to your house as we are driving." I said to her.

"Sounds good to me. I just need to shower to get my hair under control and change my outfit. I shouldn't be too long at my shop either. I just need to make sure Aria did everything for closing last night and get the small clearance table ready to go. It should really only take me an hour. Then I will be ready to go. Did you have an idea in mind for what we do today?" She asked.

"I had something in mind, yes. I thought maybe we could grab a bite to eat and take a walk down by the water. Just enjoy the day. It's cold out but not unbearable today so we can be outside if you are up for that."

"That sounds perfect. I love walking by the water. It's so quiet compared to the street I work on. Almost as if the noise is totally absorbed by the water, even though there is no sound of crashing waves. It's so still." She was looking out the window while she said words that sounded like poetry. She looked like she belonged in a movie. That perfect girl with the curly hair who loves big words and books.

"Then we will get our food to go and go sit by the water and eat. How does that sound?" I asked.

"That sounds like a dream. I could bring a book and read it to you if you would like. Besides the coffee shop, the bench right by the marina is where I like to read the most." She replied. "I like to get lost in reading because that means that everything else in my mind stops for a while." She continued. I looked over at her when she said that and there was such a sadness about her.

"I would really love for you to read to me. I never really got into reading because I always had my hands under the hood of a car with my pops. He died when I was twelve. I lost my mom a couple years after that. So I was really lost for a long time. All I wanted to do was work on the car my dad left me. I guess it was my way to feel close to him." I confessed to her.

"I am so sorry for your loss. Both of them. I lost my dad when I was a baby. I never got the chance to know him. Which I guess in a way is lucky because I don't have the pain that comes with his loss. He committed suicide. My mom wasn't the same after that, or so my grandparents say. I only know her as she is." She started to cry. "I think I get a lot of my issues from my dad. My mom always chose to ignore it because it was easier for her that way. But I really am sorry you lost them both. I'm glad you found something that brings you peace. Your car really is beautiful. Your dad would be proud." She said to me. No one has ever said that about my dad. I was at a loss for words. I know a thank you would suffice but I felt more than thanks. It was a sense of gratitude.

"I really appreciate that Olivia. I am so sorry you lost your dad. If you don't mind me asking, how did he do it? Or did you never want to know?" I asked.

"No, I asked when I was old enough to understand what he did. I couldn't get a straight answer from anyone about it. Instead of continuously prying I decided to just go to the library and search news articles. I figured someone would have wrote about it, I mean this town isn't huge and the suicide rate isn't very high. I found an article and was too scared to read it at the time. I asked the librarian for a copy to take home, I could tell she bent the rules because she pitied me. I wanted to read it in the comfort of my own bedroom." She hesitated before continuing. "So I got home with the copy of the article of my dad's suicide and sat on my bed. I know I never knew him but it was breaking me. The idea of my dad being so sad that he couldn't watch me grow up. I wanted to read it though, I wanted to know what happened. It had a blurry image of my dad covered by a white sheet on this board being carried out of the house. I wasn't sure I could read it after seeing him that way, especially displayed for the public to see." She stopped again, doing her best to hold back tears. I had begun to wish I had never asked her something like this.

"I read it anyway. He shot himself. I was apparently napping in the other room and my mom was at work. The only reason they even had access to that information is because a neighbor ran over after hearing the shot go off knowing there was a baby in the house, they called the police and then the police called my mom's work to send her home." She took a deep breath and I spoke before she could start again.

"I am so, so sorry. I shouldn't have asked you such a personal question like that. I can't express to you how awful I feel for asking you how he did it. And I am so sorry you were there when it happened. I'm grateful you were far too young to remember it. When we get to your house I would like to hug you if that's okay?" I asked.

"Yeah. I would like that. Don't apologize for being curious. We are just getting to know each other. Unfortunately for both us that means opening wounds." She wouldn't look over at me when she said that. I knew she was hurting. I knew how hard it was to talk about losing people you loved. I needed to brighten the conversation. I didn't want our parents and the past to ruin our day.

"After I lost my parents, I got Banks. He is my best friend. I didn't have any intentions in getting a dog at the time. I was lonely, sure, but I wasn't into the idea of having an animal at home that depended on me. I needed my resume to look better when I was applying to the shop I work at now and so I thought volunteering was the right way to go. I decided on the local shelter and I had only been there about a week when all of these boxer mix puppies were dropped off. I noticed Banks because he was the biggest puppy out of all of them. I picked him up and took him out in the yard to play and just fell in love with him. Now he eats what I eat and likes to sneak into my bed when I'm not home." I laughed. She laughed too, so my idea of talking about a cute baby Banks worked.

We were coming up on her house now. I pulled in her driveway and jogged around to her side of the car and opened her door. I immediately wrapped my arms around her and whispered in her ear.

"You're home now."

Number 12.

Olivia.

We pulled in the driveway of my house and I felt frozen. Talking about these things made me sad. I know I need to try to enjoy this day with him but my mood has just plummeted. He opened my door for me and scooped me up in his arms. I had never felt so safe. I actually felt like I could calm down and find the strength to pull myself up into a happier place. He whispered into my ear and I could feel my heart skip. He told me I was home. Yes, I know we are physically in front of my house but I am also in his arms. I am choosing to believe he meant I found a home within him. I felt so consumed by the smell of his skin. I looked up at him, our eyes met and I just let the words fall off of my tongue.

"Let me know you." I said to him.

"What do you mean? You do know me?" He questioned,

"I'm not talking about how much you love your car and your dog. I want to know the things that make your entire body tremble. The things that scare you into needing someone else to hold you. The things you love so deeply you keep them safe in the depths of your soul." I wanted him to share everything with me. To know him in that way would be to know his heart inside and out. The way his mind works. His favorite smell, his favorite film. I wanted to know all of it.

"I promise you, Olivia. I will share the world with you." He said.

My heart skipped again, like he could throw off the entire beat of it with the simplest of sentences. I could feel myself falling deeper into the abyss that was him. I think I know now what love really is. Honestly, it is not very complicated. Love will guide you to who you want, it will give you what you want, or it will completely destroy you. I could feel it in my bones that this would be the kind of love that would demolish me. I don't think I care, though. Why would I let something like this slip through my fingers? That would be foolish. Much more foolish than risking it all to be loved the way you could only dream of.

"I'm going to run inside and shower. You are more than welcome to come inside and wait." I said.

"I will follow you then." He replied.

"I apologize for the mess. I was going through my books because I want to bring some in to the store for people to do as a book exchange type of thing. I would have some of my books as a donation almost and people can just come and trade them out for a book they have already finished. I think it would be a neat way to get more people to read." I said as I kicked a pile of books out of the hallway back into the living room.

"I don't mind the mess. I really like that idea, too. If you would be interested, I am really handy. I could build you a large book shelf. It would wrap around your entire wall." He seemed so excited about this idea and I actually was too.

"That would be amazing. I would appreciate that so much." I could picture it now. A wrap around book shelf, a small velvet couch with an end table. Plants all around with the bay window behind it all letting in the rays of the sun. It would be such a tranquil place for me to relax. I wouldn't have to rely on the coffee shop or freeze down at the marina. I would actually have a space in my home that I could be completely free in. That may sound strange, but my house is just as messy as my mind is. It's a pretty good parallel. I tend to struggle to keep my home organized when my brain is messy too. I find myself in my bed a lot. If he is able to build me this bookshelf I would be so thankful.

"Consider it done then, miss." He said, in by far the cutest tone I have ever heard. I could see it on his face he was already planning it out in his head. He was walking the walls counting his steps. I wasn't exactly sure how that was helping him with a bookshelf but I didn't care, I liked watching him putter around.

"While you finish walking the length of my living room I am going to go ahead and hop in the shower. I am starting to run out of time." I started to turn around to go walk up my stairs and then he grabbed my arm, spun me around and kissed me. He backed away with a huge smile on his face.

"Okay, now you can go shower." He smirked.

I walked upstairs into my room and shut the door behind me. I'm not sure why I did that considering we have already slept together. I laughed it off and found my way over to my closet. I wanted to wear something simple but also something that would make him want to keep looking at me. I don't have much in the way of really nice things. So finding something that fit the idea in my head was not an easy task. I grabbed my cozy pair of tighter jeans with the cuffs at the bottom, they fit in the right places so that helps. I picked out my black flats and my off white turtle neck. I think this is a good look for our day out. I'll throw on my necklace and leave my hair flowing. I'm most comfortable with my hair down because it's easier to hide my face. I proceeded to rinse off in the shower and quickly throw my outfit on, I grabbed my jacket and head back down stairs. He was looking through the pile of books I had kicked into the living room. I couldn't hide the way that made me feel. To see this perfectly made man sitting in my living room, looking through my stack of books, after a night of sleeping together was truly unreal. I don't know how to put it into any other word than that. People like him, moments like these just don't happen to me. I haven't ever thought of myself as someone good enough for anyone so seeing him be so taken by me is hard for me to grasp.

"I'm ready to go whenever you are. You can just drop me off at the store and come back about an hour after that." I said.

"Alright, sounds good." He said as he reached for the handle of the front door. "After you, darling."

I could feel my cheeks turn red. Something about that word just gets me. He can call me darling every single moment of the day and I am just convinced I would never get tired of it. I grabbed his hand and leaned into his shoulder as we walked back to his car. I was almost sad I had to leave him for an hour to make sure my store was all set for the day. Two days ago, leaving the house to go in to work would have been the highlight of my day. He opened the car door for me again and I got in. I sunk into the seat and just took in the moments that had flown by over the last 24 hours. I was actually happy. I hadn't felt myself sink into a depressive state in a couple of days. I don't think I remember the last time I went that long without being sad. I don't remember the last time the voice in my head that said I should just wrap my car around a tree was silent. It was refreshing to not be afraid of myself for once. That thought in itself made me anxious. That voice doesn't stay quiet for long and I don't want to drag him down with me. I can't rely on him to make me happy every single day. I don't want to be that person.

We started off down the road toward town. The sun was shining and we had the windows cracked. He took out a cigarette carton out of his jacket pocket.

"Would you mind if I smoked while you are in the car?" He asked.

"No it's fine. I don't mind. I didn't know you smoked." I said, trying my best not to sound judgmental. I don't mind smoking, I just hate the smell. It's such a foul scent that sticks to you. I hadn't noticed the smell on him, though. I feel like I would have noticed it on him, in his car or at the very least in his home.

"I don't smoke often. I only do it to calm the nerves. I do my best to not do it in places I spend a lot of time. I don't like the way it sticks to the walls. Everything around you could potentially smell like that one small vice you have. I'm not a fan of that."

"I respect that." I said. "I hate that too. I don't mind the act of smoking itself but I don't like how it's a smell that just never leaves you or the space you are in."

"I hate the act of smoking if I'm being honest. It's a nasty habit. I wish I had never picked one up. Life just got hard and I didn't want to be the guy that drank too much. So I picked up a cigarette and let the nicotine take over for a bit." He said as the cigarette bounced between his teeth.

It was odd. I found it attractive on him. It made his look more intense. Like he would go to war for me. It made him seem like he could really fuck someone up if the opportunity presented itself. Which is also quite odd, I usually hate violence. He isn't really the bad boy type either, at least I don't think he is. I really don't know where this is coming from. I like the way I am around him. I keep finding out new things about myself. I am coming to realize it isn't that he is that bad boy type, it's that he brings out the dangerous side in me without even trying.

We pull up to my shop and I am not ready to get out yet. I could invite him in but I think that's too much. I need this hour to recuperate after the events of the last day.

"Pick me up in an hour?" I say as I lean in to kiss his cheek.

"I'll be here." He answers.

I unlock the front door to the store and start to check the list of things that needed to be done last night after I left. It looks like Aria did everything. I have never had any issues with her so I wasn't worried. The only time there was even the smallest sign of trouble was when her ex-boyfriend came in drunk looking for her. I politely turned him away and he left with no issue. I couldn't blame him for wanting her back. Aria was stunning. She was tall and blonde, she had enormous green eyes and a bubbly personality. She lit up every room she walked in. I really appreciate her friendship. I cannot wait to tell her everything that happened in between last night and this morning. She is the best to talk to and this will be the first time I can talk about a guy with her like she does with me. She doesn't come in until this evening though, so I will just have to share all of my stories with her on Monday.

Organizing the book table and making the signs for the day is one of my favorite things to do in the store. It's my way of being creative for the day. I make the book display so inviting, I put the books with the most interesting covers upfront so people will want to pick them up to read the back. The sign is always in big cursive letters, it lets everyone walking by know about the sales I am running and also had information on the book swap I want to try to do. I think today I am going to add a vase of flowers from the florist down the street. I love supporting the small businesses down the strip, plus flowers brighten up everything. I want to do some big greenery and off white flowers. The simplicity of that would fit my stores vibe so well.

I close up the shop for a few minutes so that I can run down the street to pick up some flowers for the table. It really is beautiful out today. It's chilly but not how it usually is in the fall. The clouds are big and are moving, which is another one of my favorite things. When you look up to the sky and the clouds are rolling. It's like getting a first class seat to watch God control the weather. I find joy in the small things in life. I don't really have any big moments to enjoy usually so I take the happiness where I can find it.

I chatted with the florist for a few minutes, her name is Anna. She opened her flower shop not too long before I opened my book store. It was simple conversation about how our shops are doing and about the weather. After we say goodbye I head straight back to the store. I want to finish everything that I need to sooner rather than later so I am ready to go when he gets back.

I pull out my keys to unlock the door and I noticed that the door was already opened. Only two employees and I have keys to this store. I began to get very uneasy. I felt like one of my worst fears was coming true. I slowly opened the door and stepped inside. Aria jumped out from behind the counter.

"I just couldn't wait to hear about how last night went so I decided to come in early." She smiled.

"You about scared me half to death. I had no idea why the door was open. Maybe a warning next time." I said while taking deep breaths.

"I'm so sorry Liv, I wasn't thinking. I was just too excited to hear about how your night was with your new man."

I was also too excited to not tell her right now so I let go of the fact that she nearly sent me into a full panic attack.

"It was incredible. He is probably the most amazing person I have ever met. I actually miss him and he has only been gone for thirty minutes. Is that crazy?" I asked.

"First of all, you telling me he has only been gone for thirty minutes automatically let me know that you slept together and you are going to have to tell me more. Second, it is not crazy at all. You never do this. You don't go on dates, you don't just fall for men. This is a big deal and you shouldn't feel crazy for feeling this way about it.

"You always know just what to say to make me feel better. I think you're right, this isn't something I ever do. I shouldn't let my anxiety get the best of me right now. I should be enjoying this." I said back to her. I need to take her advice.

"Yes, I am right. Now can we please talk about the fact that you slept with him? I need all of the details. So start talking." She laughed.

"How about I make you a deal. I need to check the books before I leave to go spend the day with Wren. So how about we make plans after work next week to have a girl's night and I can share all of the details with you then." I offered, hoping she would take the bait and let me finish up what I was doing. I was running out of time before he was supposed to come back to pick me up.

"That sounds perfect. I don't know how I am going to wait till then but I totally get it." She replied.

I gave her a hug and she left the store. I went back to the office to make sure everything was in order for the next couple of days so I could have a worry free day with Wren.

I finished up just as I heard on knock on the front door of the shop. He was back.

Number 13.

Wren.

I knocked on the front door of her store, I didn't just want to walk in and accidently startle her. I also didn't want to wait in the car and have her think I wasn't there to get her on time. I saw her turn the corner inside and walk toward the door to let me in. She swung the door open and asked if I was ready to go. I replied with a yes and we headed toward the restaurant down the street.

"Do you want to get food to go or would you like to dine in?" I offered.

"I think we should get the food to go and sit in the grass across from the marina and eat there."

"That sounds great. We will run in and place an order real quick and head down to the water then." I said.

I opened the door to the restaurant and we both sat down on the small bench that was by the hostess stand to look over the menu. I already knew what I wanted to order but I didn't want to make her feel rushed. I was ready to just sit out on the water and spend more time with her. If I was smart I would have taken that hour of free time while she was working to see if there were any boats open to rent out for a couple of hours. I should be pulling out all the stops to impress her right now. I think I haven't tried because she doesn't seem like the type of girl who wants those things or finds the grand gestures impressive. She seems to find joy in the simpler things, like sweet kisses and thoughtfulness. I liked that about her. The uniqueness of her nature is so appealing.

The door to the restaurant flew open and the wind blew her hair back over her shoulder while she was reading the menu. As the door closed back and the wind began to stop, I was hit with the smell of rosemary and lavender. Is it possible for a woman to give off a scent like that? Maybe they all do and I just never cared to notice. The more I think about it, I noticed this about her at her house not realizing it was her. I wrote it off as the scent of her home. Instead, it was the way her hair smelled. I hope I get to take this in for the rest of my life, which may seem premature but I truly cannot imagine this girl not in my life.

I just know she is mine and I am hers. I'm not even totally convinced that it is by our own free will. I do believe her, the story of the two people fated to be together in every life. There is no other explanation for all of this. I don't care if the stars brought her to me or just sheer luck, I won't let this fire between us burn out. I crave her. She is sitting next to me just deciding what to eat and I start to picture picking her up and pushing her against the wall. Kissing her is like coming up for fresh air. I want to kiss her more than anything in the world right now, but I think the best thing for me to do is at least see lunch through before leaning in.

"Are you ready to order, Liv?" I asked.

"Yeah I think I am. I couldn't decide so I'm just going to get whatever you are getting."

I laughed and we walked to the counter to order our lunch. The food here is usually ready pretty quick so I run to the restroom really fast to look at myself in the mirror and make sure I don't look too bad. Yes, I know that seems shallow but quite frankly to keep this beautiful girls attention I need to have it together. My hair is everywhere but not in an unattractive homeless kind of way, it's working for me. I splash some water on my face and walk back out to Olivia. She already had the food in her hands and she was smiling at me.

"Are you ready to head down to the water?" Liv asked.

"Absolutely." I replied.

I wrapped my fingers in between hers and we began walking down the cobble stone street down toward the marina. We talked about random things that made her laugh and I swear watching her smile was like watching the sun rise. I was so enamored by her, I could watch her just exist for hours.

We sat down in the grass and started to eat. It was an unreal sort of feeling to be sitting next to her and watching the water flow. It was such a sense of peace. A moment I wanted captured in time. To stay with me forever.

I now know why poets write sonnets. They are inspired by women like Olivia. So purely ethereal, she is limitless in the ways she makes me feel. I caught myself reaching for her hand again and closing my eyes. I wanted to do more than have this moment as a simple memory in my timeline. I wanted to remember those smells of rosemary and lavender. I wanted to remember the way the water became dewy in the tall grass around us. I wanted to remember the sweet tone of her voice. I could hear the whistling sound the brush made. The wind hit my cheek at the same moment her hand did. She ran her finger across my face and knelt closer to me, she began to whisper in my ear.

"Wren, open your eyes. They are too beautiful to be closed. Be present with me." She said.

Her words jolted my heart like a lightening bolt. Her words moved through me like the blood flows through my veins. I think this was the moment. You know, the one that people write about. The moment where the world around us became completely still. I would hand her my soul to know once and for all that I had finally found where I was supposed to be. She is my home. To know her is a privilege in itself. To love her, oh to love her. That is more than a privilege, it is the most important thing I will do in this life. I could feel my hands start to tremble. How do I tell a woman I have hardly known that I have fallen totally and irrevocably in love with her? How do I tell her that what I feel for her could shift the tides?

I need to say it. I will regret it for the rest of my life if I don't scream in this very moment that I love Olivia.

"Olivia. My eyes are open. I don't think they have ever been more open. I love you. I am so, unconditionally in love with you." The words flew from my mouth faster than I could process what I was going to say. I was uncertain on what her reaction was to what I had just said. She was just looking at me, with those beautiful green eyes. They were piercing threw me as I waited to hear a response.

"I love you too. I thought feeling that made me insane. To love you so soon. I feel like I don't really even know you. I just know that somewhere deep inside me, I have known you always. So yes, Wren. I love you."

I don't think I have ever been so taken back by words in my life. She loved me back. I wasn't going to wait any longer. I wrapped her in my arms, pulled her as close as I possibly could and kissed her. This time though, it was different. Yes, we had already slept together. Yes, we have kissed and it was amazing. Time seems to continuously stop in these moments with her. This kiss, was more than time stopping. It was as if I blacked out. There was no sound around me. The only thing that made me feel like I was still connected to the earth was her breathing into me. Images started passing behind the lids of my eyes. I knew what was happening. Olivia was right. I was seeing it, too. These two people who didn't look like us, but I knew by the feeling in my chest that they were. They were happy. We were happy. Then the images began to change. It was like a video reel playing backwards. I saw us, presently as we are. I saw the two of us again but the version from before. I could see them die. Before I could try to snap myself out of this, more pictures began to hit me. This was much bigger than I could have imagined. More than Liv knows. I saw versions upon versions of us. All the way back to what had looked to be the beginning of time. I saw two people, who did look like us, just like us. They were dressed in thin, shear clothing. He, well I, grabbed her arm and began to scream at her, I was saying things like if we didn't do what was asked of us we would owe a debt that would never be paid. That whoever this was, would never be satisfied. The image began panning over her, she was pregnant. She wrapped her arms around her stomach with tears running down her face.

"I will pay whatever debt there is to be paid. No matter what it may cost. They will not take this child from me." she said.

"Whatever the cost." He agreed.

Olivia was shaking me. I could feel myself pulling away from what I was seeing. I was relieved she was getting me out of my own head. I didn't want to experience any more. In truth, I didn't need to see it. I knew already. We choose our child hundreds of years ago. For whatever reason, someone wanted to take her from us and we gave our lives so that they could not have our daughter. I began to understand. We were still paying back this debt, each image I had been shown was of us meeting over and over again. We have continued to give our lives for our child. I chose in that second to never tell this to Olivia. She would run from me. Not because she didn't love me, but because she would find fear in our fate. I wasn't going to let her slip away from me. I could feel the pain from all of my past lives creeping into my soul. It was overwhelming. I took a deep breath and opened my eyes.

"Wren are you okay? Where did you go? We were kissing and then it was as if you had totally disappeared." She said frantically.

"I'm okay. I promise. I'm sorry if I scared you. I just got a bit dizzy and needed a moment to collect myself."

I could tell she knew I was lying. She didn't question me though. She just leaned into me.

"I'm glad you're okay. Do you need to lay down for a bit to relax? I can lay the sheet out and clean up lunch while you lay back, okay?" she said.

I felt guilty. She wasn't pushing me to tell her the truth and I knew that lying to her wasn't a smart idea. I knew I would come to regret it if she somehow found out the truth about us. We were just finding one another, we were okay and happy right now. I couldn't tell her that we had died together in every life we have shared and it wasn't due to a long and happy life together. Would she stay if she knew we were only brought together to die? I have to believe that we are in control of our fate at least enough to choose to live this time. Why else would we be shown the things we have? For all I know, Liv and I both have over active imaginations and both need sufficient rest, we aren't fated together and it was all just a day dream. There is no way to truly know. So I don't have anything to really confess to her. It was all just a dream.

"I think laying down is a good idea. Only if you will come lay down next to me, though." I smiled at her. I could see she was still worried. I wanted to make her see that everything was okay. I grabbed her hand and guided her onto the ground next to me. I laid us both down side by side. I twisted my fingers between hers and stared into her eyes. I just knew everything was going to be okay, we had nothing to worry about.

Number 14.

Olivia.

I have known Wren now for five months. Time has flown by sense he walked into my book store. We have laughed a lot, fought once, kissed more than I can count and fallen so in love.

To say I love him is an understated, unfair way to describe the way he makes me feel. He lights my soul on fire. The world love does not tell you that in the morning when we wake up, I am living for him. It does not tell you that when I fall into the darkest parts of myself, he is my ember. He is my reason. My home. To just love him would never be good enough. Wren deserves more than a mediocre word to know that I am his.

I know that I should be happy, he loves me. We are happy. The problem is, that I am not. I don't want that to be misconstrued. I am happy with him. I am not happy with myself. I haven't yet found a way to share how mentally fucked I am. It may be the fear that he won't love me anymore or the fear that he will still love me but won't know how to handle the real me. The intense panic attacks and the voices in my head telling me that there is no reason to live. I don't understand half of what is wrong with me so how can I possibly expect him to? I don't want to hide this from him though, if he walked into my home right now he would find me still dressed, sitting under the shower water. He would freak out. I should at least mention that I am going to see a shrink. I need to find some kind of control over what is happening to me. Before it becomes too severe to treat.

He is coming over in an hour or so to finish that enormous book shelf he has been building in my living room. I will just casually mention over dinner that I have an appointment this week and make it seem less serious than it is so he won't worry too much. I want him to think it's to manage it, not because it was getting much worse. This love is so fresh and new, I don't want this to ruin it. I always ruin everything. I heard the door open and shut. He's here early. I rush to get my damp clothes off and make it look like I had just hopped in the shower to rinse off before he came by. I don't feel right keeping all that is wrong with me a secret from him. I shouldn't be jumpy when he comes into my house. He is supposed to be the safest place for me. I have to get everything out in the open. I need to just accept the fact that if he doesn't want to hold my hand through it and be patient with me then he isn't who I thought he is and I shouldn't be in this relationship anyway. I take a few deep breaths and step out of the shower to wrap myself in a towel. I walk to my bedroom door and call down to him to let him know I just need to get dressed and then I will be down to join him.

I need to prepare myself for this conversation. I can feel in my heart that it is going to be okay and that I am scared for no reason but I'm still shaking despite it all. In the few months that I have been his, he has done nothing but support me and love me. Why would that change just because I have a battle to fight? I have been going through this sense I was so young, this isn't an abnormal conversation for me to have with someone. I wish losing him didn't scare me so much. If I didn't know any better, I would say that the fear of losing him could nearly kill me. What a silly thing to think, that heartache had the power to kill you. I faced something far worse every single day. I wake up and I have to tell the racing thoughts in my head to slow down and convince myself that I am not yet ready to die. I want to live, I don't understand why my mind wants me gone. Some days I feel as though I was put in a body with a subconscious that didn't belong. As if when my soul picked this real-estate, I was given things that didn't all fit together. I am a walking puzzle box whose pieces have been scattered so far there is no possible way to get them back together again. The wind will always keep one piece hidden from me. I will never be whole. Truthfully I don't think I ever was to begin with. Maybe that's fates way of playing a cruel continuous joke on me. I did something in some life that made happiness unattainable. I wish I could figure out a way to break whatever cosmic tie that binds me to such sadness. This version of me has always been kind and always kept her head down. I know deep down for whatever thing it is that I did, I deserve this pain. I just don't remember why. It feels unfair. We all grow so drastically throughout one life on this planet. Who's to say I didn't make up for whatever mistakes I have made in lives I don't remember. I believe that love knows no bounds of time, so I guess that means pain would know no bounds as well.

In between such deep thoughts I realized I had already done my hair and gotten dressed. I looked at myself in the mirror and repeated in my head that I was going to be okay. It was time to go have this talk. There was no avoiding it anymore.

"Good morning beautiful lady." Wren said to me as I walked down to meet him.

"Morning, how are you?"

"I'm better now that I'm here with you." He answered.

I wrapped my arms around him and gave him one of the tightest hugs I have ever given anybody. Just in case it's the last hug I ever give him.

"Wren, I have to talk to you about something. It's nothing you did so please don't freak out before I get to say what I need to." I said.

"Okay, are you alright?" He said while taking both of my hands.

"Honestly, no I'm not alright. That's the thing, I am never alright. I know when we first met I briefly mentioned having some issues but with us being months in to this I feel like I have to tell you everything." I was starting to shake again. I found the courage to continue talking anyway. "I am so lost. I have no idea who I am. I don't know how to want to be alive. Waking up in the morning is an enormous win for me. I had hoped meeting you would help me, give me something to make me feel okay. I really believed that love would make me feel more than this sadness. Instead I still wake up every single day wondering what the point is. There is this voice in my head that tells me day in and day out how unbelievably worthless I am. Why would I want to live if I mean so little?" I said with tears in my eyes.

"Liv, I am so sorry you feel that way. I know telling you how much you mean to me isn't what you need right now because that won't do much. I do love you. I want to help you in any way that I can. I am here to listen. To help carry the weight that becomes too much." His words shifted something inside of me. I was no longer afraid to share my demons with him. He loves me unconditionally. I am so incredibly thankful in this moment with him. He wasn't discrediting my feelings. He was embracing my words and emotions. Letting me spill into him like the coffee on our first date. I felt safe.

"Thank you for listening to me without judgement. You mean more to me than I know how to say." I said to him.

He didn't say a word after that. He simply stood up and held me in his arms. It was as if he knew words weren't what I needed. I needed comfort, words wouldn't do that for me. His touch does though. I can feel the nerves in my body calm down. It's like he's the moon in my story. Pulling my feelings like the tide and helping me release them. I never knew that another person could help me in this way. I always thought I would be handling these emotions on my own with no one to help ground me. For the first time in my life, I am expressing my sadness with my feet planted on the ground. I feel connected to my body, I don't feel separated from myself. I just need to cry. Not out of sadness but out of gratitude, out of relief. I felt for the very first time like I was going to make it out alive, at least until I am old and grey. When I don't have a choice but to go. This is what it feels like to want to live.

"I love you." Wren whispered to me.

"I love you most." I said.

Number 15.

Wren

I was holding Olivia in my arms while she wept. I wasn't sure I had done anything to help sooth her fears, until I felt her body relax into me. I felt her shift. I think she finally knows she doesn't have to be alone anymore. I may not be able to know when those thoughts fill her head or hear what they are saying to her, but I can spend every waking moment of our time together helping her realize how incredibly strong she is. I want her to see she doesn't need me to be okay. She has that in her already. Olivia wouldn't have made it as far as she had if she didn't have the fight of a lion in her soul. I am more impressed with her existence every single day. She fights her inner battles with grace. I would have never known how sad she was if she hadn't been brave enough to share it with me. I wish there was a way for me to tell her how proud I was of her without making her think that I was looking at her as smaller. The truth is she is greater than anyone I have ever met. She stands taller than I do. I would never put her beneath me to begin with, but to know every inch of her story and see her carry herself the way she does just goes to prove what I have always thought of her. She is the queen in this story. Not just mine, but everyone's. Anyone who meets her wants to be around her. She is magnetic. In the simplest of ways. Now I know why that is. She knows how hard she has to fight, so she assumes everyone else is fighting a battle as well. She remains calm and kind in all situations. Every piece of her has come together to make so much sense.

"Olivia, I need you to know something. You never have to fight any of this alone ever again. Although, you don't need me to help you fight. You are so much stronger than you give yourself credit for. I will stand with you or behind you but never in front of you. You are a warrior, darling." I said.

"I have never loved words more in my life. I don't think that Bronte could have written words so genuine. Thank you for loving me, for believing that I can conquer the world. I know that I can't, but your faith in me gives me hope." She said back to me, tears were still streaming down her face.

I wiped her tears away and kissed her cheeks right underneath her eyes. How is it possible that even when she cries she is beautiful? Her eyes may have been filled with water but they were shining none the less.

"Why don't you throw on your jacket, Liv? I'll work on the book shelf later this evening. Let's go get some coffee and walk by the water. Get you some fresh air and away from the house." I offered.

She nodded and walked to grab her coat. I took her hand and kissed her lips. I opened the car door for her and she slid in. She seemed lighter once she made it outside. I was thankful she felt like she could share all of her troubles with me. I knew there was something that bothered her deeply that she wasn't ready to speak of when we first met. Now that she finally felt like opening up to me about it, I wanted to help her become the happiest she could be. I know we have only been in each other's lives for months now, but really I have known her longer than that and that is the unspoken truth between the two of us. I know this is an insane thought to have. I know everyone around us would think we were rushing things but if the visions Olivia and I had were real, we aren't rushing a thing because we may not have that much time. I think I knew I wanted to do this the moment I laid eyes on her. I am going to ask Olivia to marry me. I made her a ring at work. I didn't think she would want a traditional diamond ring from the jewelers in town, so I decided to take metal and a small diamond and make it myself. It was dainty and simple, I used copper and bought a small uncut diamond to place in the middle of it. When it was ready I just knew she would love it. Just as untraditional as we are. She had no idea what I was planning to do today. Before she poured her heart out to me, the plan was to continue on her book shelf while she read and then take her down by the water again. I wanted to dance with her in the dark with no music. Tell that beautiful creature how much I love her and get down on one knee as I spun her away from me. The plans may have changed now that she is sad and I needed to take her out to get some fresh air and coffee. In retrospect I could still do the same thing later in the evening and she would have no idea. The way I played this proposal out in my head was everything I thought she would want, a simple moment carved out in time forever. She loves the sentiment and the poetic gestures in life. So the idea of dancing with her under the stars on the water with no music, spinning her around and getting on one knee sounded like the perfect thing to do for her. I will just have to figure out a way to keep that as my plan because she deserves all the beauty life has to offer her.

"Olivia, after we get coffee lets run into your store and grab your favorite book full of poetry and go sit by the water. How does that sound?" I asked.

"That sounds like everything I needed today. I don't know how you do it. You always know just what I need. I love you." She said to me. Liv telling me she loved me were words I knew would never get old. She reached for my hand and measured hers against mine. It was one of the most intimate things she does with me. She studies us so closely like if she blinks she will miss something important. I adore that. She makes me believe in so many things. I wish I could tell her every moment of the day without annoying her, every single detailed thing she does that makes me love her. I will just have to save all of that for my vows, if she decides to take my hand.

We walked in to grab some coffee. I threw my hand around her waist and walked in next to her. Liv ordered for both of us and we walked across the street to her store. I was looking forward to her grabbing a book of poetry to bring with us to the water. One of my favorite things in the entire world is listening to her read, especially words that slip from her tongue like honey. That is something I need to share with her. I walk up behind Liv and wrap my arms around her.

"Beautiful lady, can I tell you something?" I said as I kissed her cheek. She laughed.

"Of course." Her cheeks were getting warm from blushing.

"Listening to you speak when you read to me is my utmost favorite thing in the entire world. You speak and my entire body feels the way you do when the sun hits your skin. Warm and comforting." I could feel her start to smile and her body tightened. She turned to me and kissed me. I pulled back to see her face.

"Wren, you light my soul on fire. Don't ever stop." She said while she kissed my neck. Oh how I love this woman. I was ready to ask her to be my wife right then and there. I probably would have if Aria didn't pop her head around the corner.

"Sorry you two love birds. I didn't know you two were back here. I thought we had customers getting frisky in the poetry section. Not that I would blame them but I'm pretty sure we aren't allowing make out sessions on the books." Aria laughed.

"It's completely fine. Thank you for coming to check it out. I was just grabbing something before Wren and I head down to the water." Liv said to her.

Their friendship was a good one. It wasn't anything serious but they seemed to really enjoy one another and that is so good for Liv. She needs that, especially in someone who works in a store she loves so much.

"Careful Aria, next time you come sneaking up on us around the corner like that my pants my just be down around my ankles." I burst out laughing. They both in turn gave me this look like they were not amused by my jokes. I thought it was funny. It was the truth, I didn't know Aria was even here. It's not an unlikely scenario, Olivia and I don't keep our hands off each other too often.

"Let's get going so you can read me some of that book by the water before sunset." I said.

"You're right, let's go ahead and get going." Liv replied. She hugged Aria and we walked out onto the sidewalk. I was ready to ask her. I was beginning to get anxious, nervous even. I love this woman with every piece of me. I didn't know something like this could ever happen to someone like me. What if she says no? What if she saw more of our past and didn't share it with me? If she knew we could die if we chose one another she wouldn't marry me. I took a deep breath and let it go for now. She knows how to read me too well, she would be able to tell something was up if I didn't get my shit together. We were approaching the marina and I scooped her up and had her in my arms. She was laughing the whole time I walked us over to the tree we like to sit at. I sat her down and then I sat myself against the tree so she could slide in between my legs to read.

She began to read the most beautiful poems and I got lost in her words. I was just listening as I watched the clouds turn colors. It was almost sunset. She continued reading even as the sun went down. Poems were something that made Olivia feel something. She felt alive, like the words individually made marks on her soul. It was incredible to watch her become so engaged in what she was reading, she really allowed herself to become one with what she was seeing on the pages in front of her.

I rubbed her head as she put a bookmark in the last place she read and she leaned into my body. It was a moment of true peace. All you could hear was the wind and the water. I could feel Olivia breathing and I could hear her sighs. Nothing else around us mattered. I love that life happened that way for us. We really become so engulfed in each other that nothing else seems to matter. I am ready for this to be life forever, no matter how long or short that is. Time is irrelevant to me, with her every moment is infinite. There is no end to us. We will always find our way back to each other. My certainty in that is the one thing I cling to. I know she is mine and I am hers, no matter what fate has in store for us.

The sun has gone down and I can feel the level of nervousness rise in my chest. I stand up and stick out my hand in front of her.

"Olivia, may I have this dance." I asked as I reached down for her hand.

"There is no music, what exactly would you like us to dance to?" She laughed as she took my hand.

"Absolutely nothing. Just dance with me, baby." I held her hand in mine and my other hand rested on her waist. I pulled her in to me as close as we could possibly be and I just danced with her. It was more than I had pictured in my head. This was real, I was about to ask this woman to marry me. I was about to spin her around and my heart began to pound. I felt her arm move as she twirled away and I immediately got down on one knee. When she stopped and faced me, her reaction was everything a man could hope for. Her curls settled into place, her eyes welling with tears, a smile so beautiful and bright the stars didn't need to be shining.

"Wren what are you doing?" She said softly.

"Olivia, I have loved you sense the very moment I walked across the street into your store. You are every end and every beginning. I promise you I will cherish your heart and protect your soul. I will love you endlessly. For all of my days. Come marry me baby." I said to her, I could feel myself begin to cry. My hands were shaking and I present her with a ring.

"Yes, one million times yes." She ran into my arms and kissed me. In between each kiss she made a proclamation.

"Wren I promise I will always love you."

Followed by, "I will always make sure you know how undeniably incredible you are."

I couldn't stop smiling. Olivia wiped the tear from under my eye and held her hand out for me to put the ring on her finger.

"Do you like it?" I asked.

"It is the most beautiful ring I have ever seen. Where on earth did you find something like this?" She said.

"I made it myself. I used some of the tools at work. I thought you would appreciate the sentiment of this more so than a normal diamond ring." I explained.

"Yes oh my goodness, Wren. The thought that you put into this is so beautiful. I am so grateful to have found you. No matter if it's our fate or the stars. I love you and I will never let you go for as long as I live." She cried.

Seeing her this happy was something I will never forget. I wanted to enjoy every second of this with her but this feeling crept up inside of me. This overwhelming sense of guilt. I knew why, but she just said yes. I am spending the rest of my life with the woman I love. If I tell her the truth about us now she might take it back and I don't want her to lose this sense of happiness. I am doing this for her. Maybe there is a way for me to find out if any of what we have seen is true before I scare her. I will figure that out tomorrow. For tonight, I want to be completely wrapped up in her. We kept kissing as we made our way back into town toward my car. I wasn't convinced we weren't going to trip doing this, but I didn't care. I opened the door for her and she whispered to me something I was just not expecting.

"Drive us into the ally next to the store. I can't wait until we get home." She smiled.

I immediately hopped in the car and pulled down the side street. Before I could ask how she wanted to do this she was climbing over the center console into my lap. Liv started kissing on my neck and running her hands up my shirt. She kissed me and I could feel a smirk form on her face as she slid her hand up my thigh. This woman knows how to make me crazy. I moved my hand down the side of the seat to lay it back for us and she grabbed it before I could. She took my hand and placed it on her back. I wanted her so badly. That pure lust. For some reason, I stopped her. I brushed her hair out of her face and smiled softly at her.

"Darling, I want you just as bad. I truly do, but I just asked you to marry me. I would like to make love to my future bride in my bed. Can we finish this at home? Let me light some candles. Let me love you." I said to her.

She nodded while she tried to catch her breath.

"You always surprise me." She said.

"Life together would be far less exciting any other way." I replied.

Number 16.

Olivia

I'm lying in bed next to the man I am to marry. We just made love and he fell asleep in my arms. I should be feeling nothing but bliss. That is unfortunately not the case. I have never been so afraid in my entire life. I can feel that something about this is so terribly wrong. I am not meant for this life. The perfect story book ending with the incredible love. I was built to die. It's the devastating truth of my very existence. Yes we all die in the end, not a single one of us gets to make it out alive. I am only destined for the reality of six feet under. I accepted that a very long time ago. The moment I started hearing voices, the day I became so sad that I could not breathe. I was so young and even then I understood what fate had in store for me. The point is, if I marry him I am signing him on for such a vast heartache. That is just not fair to him. I chose to say yes, how do I back out of this now? How do I tell him I can't let him watch me die? No matter when that time is. I could get lucky and live an extraordinarily long life. I just know that no matter what it will be something that I have inevitably caused myself. I want to be happy. I want to be his wife. Wren is my mirror. We are cut from the same cloth. I can't lose him. I also can not hurt him. I don't know what I am supposed to do. My heart is ripped in two completely different directions.

Wren began to stir in his sleep. He rolled into me and wrapped me in his arms. He had started to talk in his sleep. Just little words that didn't add up to anything. All I could think was how much I love him. He deserves the world. I am too much of a disaster, he assumes that I am the epitome of happiness as I should be. Instead I am here in bed, arguing with the voice inside my head that is screaming at me to run. To get as far away from him as I possibly can. I can't shake the feeling that somehow he is the reason I don't live long. How could that be? He loves me so irrevocably. He would never hurt me. Our story is rushed no doubt, but I have known him through time and I can't imagine him doing a single thing to hurt me. I am a firm believer in trusting your intuition over your heart. So what do I do with this feeling? I surely can't ask him if he is hiding something from me. There really is no way to know why I am feeling the way that I do. There has to be a reason, I can feel my body start to shake. Being next to him is making me become uneasy. I have never felt something like this before. It was like my own energy was telling me I was unsafe. It wasn't even necessarily him, it was the two of us together.

I know this is a mistake, but I don't care. I am choosing him. I am choosing the happiness he brings me. The fact of the matter is, whatever this panicked feeling is doesn't matter. I have fully accepted my fate. My body may be making me feel afraid, my heart on the other hand is not. I made peace with whatever is to come.

I rolled over and nestled my head into his neck. I took a deep breath and let myself feel okay again. I have no control over anything that has been written for me. Whatever you believe, the stars, gods, it was set in stone for me before I set foot on this earth. Life is a losing game. I am going to make the most of it while I am here. I want to make the most of it with him. I belong to him. I can't fight it, he has taken my heart and ran away with it.

"Wren, I need to talk to you." I said as I shook him gently awake. I needed him to hear this whether he remembered it in the morning or not.

"Yes, I'm awake, what is it?" He answered, barely conscious.

"I need you to know that no matter what happens, no matter how our story begun or how it ends, it was never your fault." I laid my hand on his face as I spoke to him.

"Okay darling." He muttered.

I knew he would not remember this in the morning. That is okay with me. I just had to say it out loud. My hope is that it stays inside him so that one day, it will find its way back to the surface and he will find peace in whatever the situation may be.

I just wanted to take care of him. I love him endlessly. I find myself wishing he had fallen in love with anyone but me. To see him happy is all I could ever wish for. I just know I am far too broken to be good for him. It isn't even that I as a woman am not good enough, it is that I am mentally incapable of being healthy and stable. He says he is okay with that, but I do not believe he grasps the severity of it all.

I need to let go of these thoughts for the night, it's not fair to either of us for me to become so sad after such a special moment. I think the best thing I can do is try to shut off my thinking and get some rest. Allow myself to reboot and find continuous happiness in him. He deserves to see that I am happy that he asked me to be his wife. What an honor it is, to have this man want me unconditionally for the rest of our lives.

He is my salvation. I found my home in him. I found beauty and peace. The most insane love, in him. The purest form of ecstasy. To say I am grateful would be a gross injustice. I was barely existing before he stumbled into my life. He showed me that I could believe in something. I will never be able to thank him properly for all he has done for me. Now, we are to be married. I will be his wife.

Number 17.

Wren

I woke up this morning thankful. I looked over my shoulder and saw Olivia asleep next to me, her hair shining in the sunlight and her diamond sparkling. She actually said yes. I get to take care of this woman and love her for all of our days. I get to watch her grow as a person, help her at her bookstore. I have never been so excited for a chapter in my life to begin. While she is fast asleep I think I am going to start writing something for her. Things I do not know how to properly express.

She is embedded in every fiber of who I am. When the universe decided that it was going to be the two of us breaking the bounds of time, they made sure to leave small pieces if our pasts in each other. I believe we are connected deeper because we are able to remember. I love her completely. Forever. She is the only thing that matters here. I never realized how much of her I had memorized. I could almost tell you how many freckles crossed her face. I can tell you ever green color tone in her eyes. I can tell you how she moves when she is happy or anxious. I could write novels about Olivia. I figured she would like to read about the way I admire her. It was the most romantic gesture I could think of as a gift for her on the day we decide to get married.

I sat down to write for her and she begun to wake. I shut the notebook and slid back into bed with her.

"Good morning pretty lady." I whispered.

She gave me a sleepy smile and covered her head with the blanket. Maybe I would have time to write to her after all. Liv was not a huge morning person. She took her time getting up in the morning. I loved that about her. Slow mornings with her are a thing I cherish.

I began to write to her again. I knew what I wanted to say to her but I needed it to come out right. I wanted this to be something she can look back on in fifty years and smile over. To help her remember how much I have always loved her. I bought this notebook specifically to fit her taste as well. Its leather and is kept closed with a bronze lock. It just looked like a book that belonged on her shelf. It would blend in with every story she had but be so significant to us. I liked the idea of the sentiment. A treasure, a personal story written amongst her favorite novels.

I opened the curtains a bit more so I had sunlight to help me see better. The light hit Olivia just right. The sun seems to favor her. It always finds her features and highlights them in the most beautiful way. The glare of the sun is what lead me to her to begin with.

"Wren what are you doing over there?" I heard Liv say.

"Nothing baby, are you getting up for the day or would you like me to shut the curtain back over and you can go back to sleep?" I asked.

"I'm up for the day I think. I want to head to the store a bit earlier today. I have a lot to do." She said.

"Okay, what time do you think you will be back today?" I wanted to get some writing done for her and I had to take Banks to the park to play some today too.

"I'm not sure. It's just me today so I will probably be there until eight o'clock maybe eight thirty. I am going to go to my place tonight too, I need clothes." She said, she was pulling her hair back and throwing on her clothes from the day before. I didn't want to sound over bearing so I decided not to ask if she wanted me to take her to work.

"Do you want me to come over later tonight?" I was hoping she would say yes. After all, we just got engaged. I wanted to spend time with her.

"Not tonight. I am going to go home and read. I might take a bath. I just need some time." She wouldn't look at me. Her demeanor completely changed.

"I understand, love. If you change your mind just give me a call okay?" I said to her hoping she would open up to me at least a little.

"Yeah absolutely. I just haven't spent any time at home by myself lately." She answered.

I walked over to her and grabbed her hand. I kissed her cheek and looked into her eyes.

"Olivia, are you alright?" I asked.

"Yes everything is fine. It isn't anything you did. I just need a breather, you know? We are so serious and have been sense the day we met and that's fine, I just need to be with myself for a moment." Olivia said.

I understood what she was saying. We did move fast and do spend a majority of our time together. I get it, I just hope she isn't second guessing saying yes.

"I understand. I hope you enjoy some time to yourself tonight. You deserve to relax." I said to her.

She smiled up at me and wrapped her arms around my neck. She kissed me and walked out the door.

She hopped in her car and drove off to work. I stood in the doorway for a moment. I feel like I need to tell her about what I saw. That her and I might not live if we stay together. I have it in my head that any time she comes off distant it is because she can tell I have been hiding something from her. I also am very aware that if I do tell her that she will leave me. I need to stop overthinking. She has no idea what I have seen. I still don't know if it's real. She just needs time to herself. We all need that sometimes. I just need to remind myself that everything is just fine and she loves me.

I grabbed Banks leash and his favorite ball so we could go out to the park. I haven't been playing with him as much because most of my time has been spent doing things with Liv. I could tell he knew we were going somewhere, he starts wagging his tail so hard I am almost certain he could put a hole in the wall. I called him to follow me and we went out to the car. I roll the window down halfway for him to stick his head out. He loves to bite the wind when we go for a drive.

On our way to the park I thought I would stop in to check on Olivia. It had been only an hour of her being gone but she just left so suddenly this morning I wanted to know she was okay. I just want to drive by and see that she is smiling.

Number 18.

Olivia

I liked the decision to come in this early to start things at the store. I have more time to organize books and check on things before I turn the sign to open. It is giving me more time to process. I couldn't stop thinking about how fast I left this morning. I felt bad for just rushing out on him. The truth is, the thoughts from the night before had not stopped. I was very unsure on if marrying him was the right thing to do. I didn't want him to know that yet though. I would say something to him when I was entirely sure as to what the right thing to do was.

I felt myself sinking into this deep state of depression. I loved this man, but the voice in my head kept yelling at me to die. Wouldn't it be easier if I just ended things? People look at me from the outside and see this pretty girl who owns a book store, who has this perfect man to love her. On the inside though, I am rotting. I don't want to have to make the decision on if I am going to marry him or not. I don't want to think about our fate. The things we did or didn't do to get here. I just wanted it to stop. The overthinking, the visions, the voices, the sadness that is utterly destroying me. I am just done. I don't want to have to fight to breathe anymore. It is just a silly concept. From the outside looking in, I have everything. On the inside I am so broken. I know I told him I would go get help and that it wasn't that bad. I thought I was at a point where talking to someone could save me. I no longer think that is the case.

I was fiddling with some books when I noticed Wren pull up outside. I couldn't let him see me like this. I was a wreck and was not ready to explain myself to him. I didn't want to ruin his day. I made myself look content and busy so maybe he would keep driving. My plan looked like it was working. He had Banks after all and he wouldn't leave him in the car.

I hate how my mind works. I am so conscious about the things I think. I can fight the voices and tell myself that I am okay one minute and the next minute I am ready to jump off the bridge at the marina. I have been close before, but never like this. Not when I have something to live for and still want to end it all. I thought that being with Wren would make me have something to hold onto. I thought loving him would convince me to live. Instead, it has given me more of a reason to die. It saves him from having to live a life with someone so damaged without either of us having to make that choice. The idea of it all finally stopping is so relieving. No matter voices, no more intrusive thoughts, no more fighting. It would just be quiet.

I didn't want to do this in some dramatic way. I didn't want to do it in some gruesome way that would scar anyone. That isn't fair to do to another person. I had an idea. I was ready. I had always accepted this part of me. I had some things to get in order first. I wanted to leave the store in Aria's hands. I wanted to make sure that Wren knew I loved him. I didn't want to just disappear. The people I cared about deserved something to have when I am gone. I didn't have much to give but I needed to know they could be okay. I did love them, I loved him. I just needed the pain to end.

I am going to have a good last day. One that I remember, if there is somewhere I get to go where I can remember it.

I think I am going to grab my favorite book, "Little Women" and walk to the marina. Get myself some flowers and close the store for the day. I am going to get a hold of Wren and have him meet me later this evening for coffee. Do all of my favorite things and end it with my favorite person. Then I can finally write the words "The End' in my story. My soul will finally find some peace. For the very first time I was walking around fearlessly. I could feel it inside of me, this was the best decision I can make for myself. My trauma is too deep to heal. I am far too shattered to fix. There is peace in this form of acceptance.

I picked up my bag and my book and headed down the street to the flower shop. I grabbed some baby's breath and some lavender. I wanted to have a small memorial for myself. An intimate thing for just me, to show gratitude for fighting as long as I did and for letting myself love him the way I have.

I walked toward the water and sat on the bench. I flipped to my favorite chapter and read it over and over again. I absorbed these words into my skin. I would never forget them. I picked up the flowers and set them on the edge of the water by the rocks. I wasn't going to say anything out loud but I decided I deserved to do this properly.

"Olivia Marie Beck, you have given this life everything you have. You have fought beautifully with the strength of a warrior. You lived to see your twenties. You lived your dream of owning your own book store. You fell in love, in such a way it was hard to believe it was real. You should be so proud of yourself. You have lived through things no one should ever have to endure. You don't have to fight anymore, sweet girl. You deserve this rest." I said, realizing I was saying goodbye to myself. I began to cry. I was sad because it hurt to know I had been suffering for so long, but the tears were for the fact that I was finally ready to do this. I knew I was going to go somewhere beautiful. God was ready to welcome me home. My dad was there waiting for me. I could picture the barley fields and the never ending golden hours.

I needed to find Wren and ask him to meet me in a couple of hours for coffee. I guess I will go wait for him at his house and then head to mine once plans have been made. I walked back to the store and got in my car. I have to decide what I was going to say to him. How do you sum up how much you love someone in a matter of sentences so they don't question it once you are gone? I will just pour out my heart and kiss him as hard as I can because it really will be my last time.

I roll the windows down and take in the wind and the sun light on my skin. It is amazing how much we take for granted on a day to day bases.

I pull into Wren's driveway. He is already back home with Banks. He steps out from the garage and walks over to my car. He opened my door and helped me out.

"Hey darling, I wasn't expecting you here tonight. Especially not this early. Is everything okay?" He asked me.

"Yes baby it is. I just don't have a phone at the store and wanted to know if you would meet me in town for coffee in a couple of hours?" It was hard to talk to him and hold back tears. My throat started to burn. I knew how badly this was going to hurt him.

"Yeah absolutely. I will finish up the car and hop in the shower. I will meet you there okay?" He said back.

"Wren before I leave I just want to say something to you. I am sorry for how quickly I left you this morning. I just had so many emotions rushing through me. I love you, okay? You are the absolute best part of who I am. I cannot thank you enough for loving me the way you have. It is beautiful and raw. It is honest. I hope you know that I love you the very same way." I said, resting my hands in his.

"I know you do, Liv. Are you positive everything is alright?" He asked.

"I can honestly say for once I do feel alright. I am going to be okay." I said, I looked into his eyes for a moment and leaned in to kiss him.

When I leaned into his lips, I was given a reel of memories again. This time though, they were our present memories. I was seeing the day we first met, how it felt to choose him, to kiss him for the first time. It was beautiful to relive those moments as I kissed him for the last time. I stepped back and told him I loved him one more time. He walked back into the garage and I studied every move he made, I would never forget him either. Not a single detail would go unnoticed in my memory. I sat back in the driver seat. I had to take a few deep breaths before I headed home. I knew this was the last time I would step foot at his house. I was starting to get a bit sick to my stomach. All the things I experienced here were so perfect and I was sad to know I would have no more. I put the car in reverse and drove home. I didn't like that I was starting to second guess my decision to die. I wanted this. It was healthy to be sad over the things I was leaving behind. My life may have been full of hardship but there was still beauty in it.

I stared at the clouds and watched every one pass as I drove by. I was finally at home. I walked in my front door slowly. I ran my hands over the handle, I touched each book on my shelf in the living room. I watered my plants for the very last time. I grabbed a glass of water from the kitchen and took my last sips of a drink. I let my fingers feel each grain of wood in the railing on my way up the stairs. I lit some candles and got in the shower. Each drop of water felt like pins hitting my skin. I felt like I needed to scream. I let out the loudest yell I could. I held myself and just cried. I wish things had been different for me. That I was born without the burden of a mind who hated me. I brushed my teeth, I ran the comb through my hair and put a small amount of makeup on when I was done in the shower. I picked out my favorite jeans and my softest flannel. I slid them on and sat on the edge of my bed. I decided not to lay down, I was going to be doing that permanently now.

I walked over to the hall closet and grabbed the bottle of pills. I figured this would be the best way to go. I was shaking as I opened it and poured the capsules into my hand. I knew if I waited much longer or saw Wren before taking them that I may back out. I couldn't let myself do that again. I walk back into my room and sit back on my bed. I pick up my glass of water and begin taking as many as I can. I don't know how long this will take truthfully. I am hoping I make it to Wren before it all goes dark. I don't want to die anywhere else but with him. I start to get jittery and scared. I need to make it to him. I stumble down the stairs unaware that I am leaving my house for the last time, ever. I get in my car and started speeding down the road. I could feel things getting fuzzy and I was terrified that I wouldn't find my way into his arms in time. I was starting to wish I hadn't taken them. That I had chosen differently. At least how it ends. I don't want to be driving this scared.

I want to know my life ends with him.

Number 19.

Wren

The sun was setting, it was this dark orange hue almost as if the world around me was on fire. Olivia called me a couple of hours ago to have me meet her in the parking lot of her favorite coffee shop. It's actually our favorite coffee shop. It's such a simplistic little place to sit and have real conversations with people. The lighting is dim and the walls are dark. The mood is set the moment you step inside. I think that's why she loves it so much, she loves a dark aesthetic. I decide to get out of my car and lean up against the hood to smoke a cigarette while I wait. Smoking is my biggest vice, besides her. I haven't had one in months but the feeling rising in my stomach made me feel like it was a good night to enjoy one. It was starting to get chilly out. I went to grab my flannel out the passenger side of my car but then I remembered Liv took it with her this morning. I guess that means I'll be cold until she gets here. I still don't complain when my clothes go missing because she took them, it makes me happy that she wants to wear them. I can tell it gives her comfort when she gets anxious throughout her day. I keep checking the clock that sits on the street outside the coffee shop because she was supposed to be here fifteen minutes ago. It isn't like her to run late without letting me know. The sign on the door of the coffee shop is now lit up in neon, "The Bean" is reflecting off the side of my car. I can't lie, it would be a really cool picture. The kind you want on your wall, you know? A piece of my beautiful car and our favorite coffee shop all creating one unique image. Olivia would really appreciate art that looked like that. She loves different perspectives and sentimental items. I wish she would hurry up and get here so that I can show this to her before the light isn't hitting it right anymore. Plus its getting dark and the snow just melted which means the black ice will probably be bad on the roads tonight and I would rather us not be driving on it if we can help it. I wish there was a way to find out what is taking her so long. I decide to not worry so much and light another one. I check my hair in the side mirrors of the car, it was nice and wavy this morning and I thought it would impress her, even though we have been together for quite a while it's still nice to impress her. My hair has been taken over by the wind and is no longer parted nicely, which blows. I love the way her face lights up every time she sees me. She doesn't even realize she does it half the time because it's a look she gets in her eyes and the way she smiles, it is a natural reaction. Which makes it ten times more attractive to me. To know this girl cares about me that much after all this time. I see headlights brighten over the tiny hill leading up to the coffee shop.

I think Olivia is finally pulling up. Except this car is flying and she doesn't drive like that. I'm tempted to move my car with how fast this person is driving, they are swerving all over the place. The car slides sideways and comes to an abrupt stop, before I could even react to how wild this person just flew in I realized it was Olivia. The car door flung open just as fast as she had been driving. She is terrifying me. I don't like the way this feels. She doesn't ever drive unsafe and doesn't react in a panicking way in public. When she walked around the front of her car it was like watching her move in slow motion, I was studying her to see if she was okay. I immediately knew something was absolutely not okay. Her eyes were dark, blood shot even. She didn't light up when she saw me this time. She had mascara under her eyes and down her cheeks. Her chest was moving up and down faster than I have ever seen, like she was breathing for more than herself. She looked like she was trying to say something to me but the words weren't making it out. I wanted to run to her but it was like my feet were cemented to the ground. Seeing Olivia in that state had me stunned. I don't understand what is happening. As I watch her take slow steps in my direction, she started to walk sideways. Her left shoulder was dropped down like she was distributing weight somewhere else. Maybe she was drinking. I am going to be so fucking mad at her if she drove this intoxicated. My eyes don't leave her as she moves. She is stumbling over her feet, still crying. I need to know what's happening to her.

"Liv, are you okay? What is going on? Have you been drinking?" I started to talk in a panic.

"No. I haven't been drinking Wren. I am so sorry. I'm sorry. I need you to forgive me. Don't hate me, okay? I love you. I love you more than I knew was humanly possible." She was almost screaming these words at me. What is she apologizing for? If she wasn't drinking why is she in this state? I just can't figure out what is happening right in front of me.

"Alright Liv, it's all alright okay. Just come sit with me on the car. Let's get some fresh air and talk about what is going on." I need her to breathe and relax because I can tell as she gets closer to me that she might very well pass out.

"There is nothing left to talk about baby." She is sobbing at this point. My sweet girl looks so broken and I don't know how to help her this time. I haven't ever seen her like this, honestly I have never seen anyone like this before. I went to step forward into her and help her sit down. She needed something to drink. I'm just going to sit her on the curb right here and then go inside the coffee shop and grab her a cup of water, that'll help.

Before I could step into her, she collided into me. I went to move her back and move the hair out of her face but something changed the moment she landed in my arms. She wasn't moving. She went limp. I sat on the ground and held her. She opened her eyes and looked up at me. The relief that came over me was unlike anything I have ever felt.

"Wren, I can feel myself leaving my body behind. I am dying. I am so sorry, I love you." She could barely get the words out.

I started to hyperventilate. She couldn't have really done this, right? This beautiful woman in my arms would not hurt me so deeply as to die in my arms. This can't be real. This isn't real, I have to be having a vision again. One that is showing me what will happen if I don't tell Olivia what could happen if we get married.

"Look at me." She said as she reached for my face. "This isn't on you. I just needed it to end. I was tired."

"Olivia no. You promised me you were okay. I love you. Don't you leave me, I am going to find help." I said to her.

"Baby, don't walk away. We are out of time. Hold me." She whispered. Her body went limp again.

I felt her let out a long breath and then nothing. She stopped moving. There was no movement coming from her chest. She wasn't breathing.

"Come back to me baby!" I am screaming. "Hold on okay, don't you leave me. I need you. Just hold on."

I can't lose her. She can't be gone. This wasn't supposed to happen. I wrapped my arms around her body.

"Olivia don't you fucking leave me. You promised me you would stay."
She said she was getting better. She swore to me she was going to be alright. I can feel her body change while I hold her. Is this what death feels like? What it looks like? She still looks like her. Her eyes are still a beautiful emerald green. Her skin is turning pale but not much more than her normal color. It is just different. How do I live without her? Without her arms, her face, her smile. I lightly touch her cheek with my finger tips and grab her face.

"Olivia, you promised me baby. I need you to hold on to me. You can't be gone."

I don't know what to do. I want her to open her eyes. To look at me and tell me she is okay. As time keeps slipping by in what seems like years I realize that the love of my life, my home, she is just gone.

I can't go on like this. Not without her. There is no light without her, there is just darkness. If she is gone, I am leaving with her. I made a promise to her too.

That I would stand behind her to watch her rise. She rose. She is gone now. It is time for me to follow behind her.

I laid her down gently next to my car. I opened the door and let my hand fall into the center console. I felt my hand brush the metal. My adrenaline was pumping and my heart felt like it was going to fall out of my chest. I was becoming too numb to Olivia being gone to be afraid to die.

I just needed to make this quick. I didn't want to be here another second without her. I walk over to sit next to her. I kissed her forehead. I racked the slide and watched as my bullet was taken into the chamber. I reached down and squeezer her hand. I looked at Olivia one more time as I raised the gun to my head. I wanted to take in her beauty. I love her. I kept my fingers intertwined with hers as the sound of the safety broke the silence. It was time to follow her.

"I'll see you soon."

Part Two.

Another year.

Another life.

The same fate.

Number 1.

Tatum

Today I woke up undeniably happy. The snow is sparkling and the air is chilled. The sun is shining perfectly through my window, it is highlighting the red hues in my curls. I am grateful for mornings like this. The natural light makes me feel beautiful. My eyes glitter their hazel tones. My freckles dance across my face. I want to start my day slowly. To practice some self-care and drink a hot cup of coffee. I grab my tan silk robe and the softest blanket I own and walk over to my antique velvet green chair in front of my window. I grab the book I am currently reading off the shelf as I pass by. I just want to soak in today.

There is a feeling welling up inside of me, telling me that today will be extraordinary. Most days I romanticize my life. Life should be lived as if you are the main character in the story of the universe. It is too beautiful a world and a life we have been given to live it ordinarily.

I pick out one of my favorite outfits to wear out just to impress myself. I grab my black long sleeve crop top, by plaid high waisted pants, black boots and all the gold jewelry I own. My hair is wildly curly and I make sure my eyebrows are done and my eye bags are covered. I feel quite pretty.

I think I am going to head to the vintage book store in town today and buy another novel to add to my ever growing collection. Although it is 2018, I refuse to buy a digital device to read my books on. I find too much joy in the smell of a new book, to feel the pages underneath my fingertips. Some of the things that make you happy cannot be turned into a modern convenience. There will never be a comparison between reading a book on a screen that ruins your eye sight and going to a book store to hand pick a book that speaks to your soul. A novel to sit upon your shelf when you are finished as a memory of the numerous lives you have lived. No one will ever be able to change my mind on that. There is no argument good enough. Books are a way for the people who wrote them to live infinitely and for their stories to be shared throughout years. If you download a book onto a computer or tablet, that book can disappear with the shatter of a screen. Therefore, I will forever buy my books off of shelves in stores ran by small owners in small towns.

After I adventure into the book store, I think I will go to the bakery next door to it and buy some lavender cakes to take back home with me. My studio isn't much, but it is home. I love to spend my time sitting in my window watching the people below. I tend to create fictional lives for them as they pass by. You know, when two lovers walk by laughing I imagine they are laughing because they are on a first date with one another and the awkwardness shared between them is just truly comical. It keeps my occupied when I'm not nose deep in a book. I have off the rest of the day so I am going to take my time. I have nowhere to rush off to. I do enjoy my job don't get me wrong, I just stay so busy pouring coffee for people and doing school work that I don't find time to just allow myself to slow down and find some peace within the day.

New books in hand and the smell of fresh pastries truly was just the best way to start my day of bliss. I got to have a slow morning, indulge in my favorite small things and I am truly, genuinely giddy. I don't think I could have asked for a better day. The snow is perfectly white and has yet to be covered in black soot from people's cars, the air is cold but there is no wind. The earth is just silently still. I stop moving for a moment to take a deep breath and let the warm sun hit my face. There isn't really anyone out and about this morning seeing as the snow storm just hit yesterday evening. It is so quiet I can hear the snow make that crackling sound underneath my feet as I walk. I have officially seized my day.

I arrive back outside the building where my little studio apartment resides and I was so enamored by the way my day is going I just wasn't ready to go inside yet. I could walk to campus and see what people are up to over there but truthfully I think that would ruin my day, campus life is the exact opposite of peaceful. Especially on a snow day, which also happens to be a Friday. I can just imagine walking through the brick gates of campus and seeing all the frat boy's hauling snow balls at one another. I needed a far better plan than that. I have already done my favorite things, I don't need to go shopping. I have bills and tuition to cover before I go buy a new skirt. I don't want to go to the tavern either. I think I better just go inside. If I try to venture too much I may just destroy the perfection that has been my morning. After I spend some time in the comfort of my home maybe I can think of something to do later. For now though, I am going to start my new book, eat my little cakes and light some candles. I will continue to be my own peace today.

Number 2.

Rhys

I rolled over in bed not even totally sure I have slept at all. The sun is up and the snow has completely blanketed the ground. I sit up and look over at myself in the mirror. I am not exactly pleased with the reflection I see. My hair is sticking out in every direction, the bags under my eyes are so purple I look like I got into a fight and to be completely truthful I look like the walking dead. I am so glad I live alone and not in the dorms anymore because I can guarantee I would have scared the shit out of someone this morning. I really look like a corpse, it's gross. I am already so pale and my eyes are a dark brown so I don't have much going for me to begin with. I need to get up and shower this funk off of me. There is no way I am going into work this morning looking like this. I don't care much about my appearance but I care enough to not scare a small child into believing I am the monster they think is hiding under their bed.

I turn the shower water on hot and brush my teeth. I grab my phone and put on my favorite playlist and start to rinse off. I start to make a to-do list in my head to help me get through the day. I know I need to go get some groceries after work because my fridge looks like no one lives here. Maybe I will go to the tavern across from the college campus this evening too. I could get a few drinks and play some pool with college kids I have no business hanging out with. We may all be about the same age but we are in two completely different places in life. They are all smart and driven, I am perfectly content with working my life away. I never had the desire to go to a university. It wasn't ever a plan I had for myself. I moved to Boston after high school and decided to buy a motorcycle. To re-invent myself, have this bad boy persona and work in a motor shop in the city. I needed that fresh start. Although it was the right choice for me, it is lonely not really knowing anyone out here. I have lived out here for years and only have one friend. Which is okay, it allows me to be freer I think.

I step out of the shower and throw on my raggedy jeans and my work tee. I slide on my boots and grab my black leather jacket. I will just stop in town to grab breakfast this morning and bring it to work with me. I didn't really have anything to make anyway. It's a lot chillier out today, I forgot it snowed again last night. The down side to solely riding a motorcycle is driving it on fresh snow and ice. I can't call out today though, I need the money. I can't afford to lose this job. I don't mind the reckless nature I carry, it keeps life more interesting.

I hop on my bike and ride off down the road. I love the view on my ride to work, I pass right through the downtown college area. There are large bulb lights strung up all over, fire pits, and small shops everywhere. It's a pretty place to live. As I go down this street, I see this woman. She looks my age, maybe twenty three. She has long red curly hair, her skin looks like silk and I can say with all honesty I have never seen someone so captivating. If I didn't know this road so well I very well may have crashed staring at her. She hasn't looked up from the ground yet so she definitely has not noticed me. I don't care though, because I see her. She carried herself so confidently and dressed so behind her time. What an insanely unique creature. I wanted to know her. She has to go to school here. She looks like the academic type. I guess that settles it, I am going to the tavern in town after work tonight. I will find her again. I have to know her.

My day began to drag by after seeing her. I was replaying the way she walked down the sidewalk in slow motion in my mind while I worked. I felt as though I knew her already but I know that I don't, I would never have forgotten someone like that. It's a strange feeling. I live in Boston, I am around beautiful women all of the time. There is something so distinctly different about her.

I stare at the clock as if it would make the time go by faster. I don't have that much longer, I just wanted my shift to be over now. I wanted to explore downtown in the hopes that I will bump into her. A girl like that is probably with someone already. That or she is so insanely independent that she doesn't need anyone to make her happy. Day dreaming about a woman you don't know is a dangerous game to be playing. I start to create an image that slowly becomes her in my mind and then that is how I expect her to be. Which is unfair to everyone involved.

I count my lonely blessings this evening. No one in this town really knows who I am, which means I will go uninterrupted while I go to different places tonight hoping to find her again. It is a Friday night after all. My chances of bumping into her rise exponentially on a weekend filled with snow. Everyone has off of classes and more free time to go out and be the ravaging young adults that they are.

I should run home first to get cleaner clothes before I head out for the night. I don't want to meet her covered in oil and grease. Some girls are into that look but I can tell she is not one of those women. She is too graceful. She wouldn't judge me for it but she wouldn't let me touch her either. I need to grab a flannel and dark stained jeans, run my hair under the water and throw on my vans. I do not want to look like I am trying too hard but I want to catch her eye too.

I am ready to throw myself into her story.

Number 3.

Tatum

I am not sure how I managed to finish this entire, brand new book but I did. It sucked me in and just like that I have puffy eyes and the sun is going down. I am not complaining though, to spend the day reading a story is never a waste of time. I really have let today be the most relaxing recharge. I am thankful to have slowed down some. I think my mind, body and soul all needed me to do it. I was becoming too sluggish. I am feeling so much better now. I think I am going to go to the tavern later. I deserve to finish out my day strong. I will dress cute, buy myself a drink and let loose for a little bit longer. I wanted to be out around people, I spent a sufficient amount of time alone this afternoon.

I considered calling my friends to head out with me in a bit but I think I am going to see the kind of people I feel drawn to tonight instead. I love meeting new people. Especially drunk college kids, we are a different breed. Honest and fun in our rawest form. Alcohol is funny that way. It removes the masks and the filters. It is my absolute favorite way to meet people. There is something about hanging out with people you do not know in a free environment that forms the most beautiful friendships.

I slid into a tight turtle neck and a black corduroy overall dress. Added some thick gold rings and my favorite gold necklace, sprayed my hair down with some water so my curls were bouncy and touched up my makeup. I was genuinely thriving today, I felt myself sprouting a new blossom inside of me. I have that basic bitch tattoo on my wrist that reads "carpe diem" and I considered getting it covered up until I realized I begun using it as a reminder to really seize each and every day. I loved the woman I was growing into. I spent so much time hating who I was that finding this new sense of self was a gift. I was proud of the girl I saw in the mirror now instead of being disgusted by her.

I looked out the window at the people rushing around below, all heading out to enjoy their snowy Friday evenings. I was ready to join the hustle and bustle. I wanted to let my guard down a bit and let myself be hit on by a man, or a woman. I don't have a preference. I haven't allowed myself the time to get into even a fling with anyone because I needed to stay focused. I had no time for distractions. I was quite content on my own as a matter of fact. Tonight though, I was feeling a hookup. I wanted to have some fun. This day deserved a lust filled ending. I looked beautiful, I felt confident so there was no reason why I shouldn't allow myself this bit of emotional and physical freedom.

The tavern wasn't crowded yet as I walked through the doors. It was loud but not so loud that you couldn't hear yourself think. The atmosphere was nice, easy to vibe with this evening. I decide to order a drink and sit on the bar stool that looks out the front windows. I liked people watching. People are so truly fascinating. Everyone has their own personality, aesthetic, type and distinguishing feature. I, for example look like I have brown hair until the sunlight hits it and all of the sudden it is on fire with orange. I never dye my hair because of that. My natural orange curls set me apart. It fits who I am. It is my distinguishing trait. I guess the insane amount of freckles I have that rest over my nose and under my eyes could be that trait as well. My hair is definitely the eye catching quality though. I was so zoned into my own little world I didn't even realize someone had come and sat down beside me. I looked over at him and immediately made eye contact. It made my stomach sink. I had too many butterflies fluttering around inside of me. I did not know how to react. What is a girl to do when she instantaneously locks eyes with a beautiful stranger? Opening my mouth and having words come out would probably be a good place to start. I reached out my hand to introduce myself to him.

"Hi, I'm Tatum. And you are?" I said smiling at him.

"Tatum. What a beautiful name. I'm Rhys. It is so nice to meet you." He replied, shaking my hand right back.

He was gorgeous. His hair was dark, so were his eyes. He dressed nice, he gave off this bad boy vibe and I loved it. Leave it to me to attract the tall, dark, toxic stranger in a bar.

"What brings you in tonight? Just out for a drink?" I asked.

"Yeah, something like that." He said back.

His voice was so deep. I swear it was a whole octave lower than most guys I have known. I need to get a couple more drinks in me before I could comfortably flirt but I didn't want him to lose interest until I reached that point. I just need to take deep breaths, subtly that is. I need to be myself.

"So Rhys, do you live around here? I don't think I have seen you around campus before." I said trying to come off a little flirty. I am doing my best anyway.

"I actually don't go to school here. I work in a bike shop down the road. I have lived in Boston sense I was eighteen though." He said, he was fumbling with his hands. Maybe I made him nervous.

"That's cool! Do you ride a motorcycle too or just work on them?" I asked, playing with my curls.

"I do, actually. You ever been on one?" Did this man just ask me if I have been on the back of a motorcycle before? Was that his way of asking if I wanted a ride? My mind is racing. I can feel my face getting hot.

"I haven't, no. No one around here really drives anything because we all live on campus, or close enough to it that we don't need a vehicle or motorcycle, I guess." I was losing my words. I felt so silly rambling like this.

"I could take you for a ride if you'd like? Maybe we get a couple more drinks and then head out for a bit?" He offered.

My heart was pumping, nearly out of my chest. Of course I wanted to get on the back of a bike with him. What a dream. He is a dream.

"Is it safe in the snow? I mean, yes of course I would love to go for a ride. We absolutely should." I answered hastily.

He started to laugh at me. At least I was humoring him with my nonsense. I just felt embarrassed. I have a 4.0 grade point average, am going to school to become a writer and I am easy on the eyes. Yet I can't get my shit together to impress this man.

"I will keep you safe. I promise." He said.

That was it. He had my heart. How is that even possible? I try so hard to be a realist and not a hopeless romantic. It's how I keep my head on straight and focus on school. He said those words to me and I just melted. It felt so natural to feel this way for him so quickly. Almost as if I knew him already. Which I knew for sure I did not. I would remember meeting someone like Rhys. I can't shake the feeling though. It was the oddest sense of déjà vu.

"We haven't met before have we?" I asked him.

"I was going to ask you the same question. I feel like I know you but there is no way I would forget you if I had met you before." He answered.

We just looked at each other for a moment. There was something intense between us. I could feel it in the deepest parts of me. He was more than a random guy at bar. I don't know if this feeling is good or bad, right now it is just overwhelming.

He walked over to the bar and grabbed us both a drink. Drinking and talking definitely lightened the mood, things were comfortable and fun. His laugh was so infectious. I had to laugh because he was. We both reached for our drink at the same time and our hands touching sent sparks through my entire body. I was ready for this bike ride now. I wanted to feel that freedom with him.

"You want to take me on that ride now?" I asked.

He smiled at me and nodded. I grabbed my purse and jacket, he reached out for my hand and we began to walk outside. We got to his bike which was beautiful, it was matte black all over with a touch of this dark, sage green. He handed me his helmet and gestured for me to get on. I could feel my nerves start to shake. I gave myself over to the moment and got on the back of his motorcycle.

We started flying down the roads so fast I felt like I walked down these streets in slow motion. I wrapped my arms tighter and tighter around his waist. I looked up and the snow was starting to fall again. I felt like I was in a movie. I am on the back of a not so mysterious man's motorcycle, soaring down streets I have only seen one way, it is snowing and sticking to my hair. I am so incredibly free in this moment. I have never felt anything like this before. He went to make this sharp turn and as my adrenaline began to pump something came over me. I saw these reels of images flash right in front of my eyes. I saw these two people, one girl and one guy. I could feel how much they loved one another. She was beautiful in this simple way, he was handsome almost like Rhys is. I feel like I am watching small pieces of someone else's life. All of the sudden the love I was feeling turned to pain. I watched them both die. I let out this scream. Rhys slammed on the breaks and we slid in the snow. He turned around so fast and looked at me.

"Are you alright? What just happened?" He asked me frantically.

I knew what had just happened. I could feel it inside of me. I did know him. Those people I saw inside my head, they were us. I read about something like this once. My mother told me about it, the way people can be tied together in each life. She would know what to say right now. I needed her advice.

"Yes I am so sorry. I'm okay. Something came over me when we were riding and it startled me." I answered.

"As long as you are okay. Would you like me to take you home?" He said.

"That would be nice, thank you. I could definitely use some coffee right now. You are welcome to come in when we get there for a cup if you would like." I offered.

"That sounds great." He said, taking my hand and helping me get back on his bike.

I know that I need to tell him, he needs to know his feeling of knowing me was in fact true. I also know that I should call my mom first. She will know how I should address this. She is all but an expert in this kind of thing. Energy is her second nature. Before my shift tomorrow I need to make sure I get ahold of her so she can walk me through this. As of right now, I am truly and utterly terrified of the images I just saw.

Number 4.

Rhys

I really pulled this off. Tatum has her arms wrapped around me and is on the back of my motorcycle. I am taking her home and she has already invited me in for coffee. This went so much better than I could have ever expected. Except for her scream. It shattered part of me. It didn't scare me, it made me feel guilty. I have no idea why her scream would make me feel something like that but it did. I can feel it in my chest that knowing her is going to end badly. For tonight though, I do not care. One night spent with her couldn't possibly hurt either of us.

We arrive at her place. It is this dark brick building with tons of lights outside of it. We get into the elevator together and head up to her door. When we walk in its kind of funny, it is exactly what I thought it would look like. It's clean and organized, books everywhere, dark tones and a velvet chair in the corner by her window. She is definitely true to herself. I liked this about her.

"How do you like your coffee?" Tatum asked.

"Black, please." I answered

"I kind of assumed so but you never know." She said laughing at me.

"Now why would you assume I drink my coffee without cream?" I asked, smiling at her.

"You just don't come off as the guy who likes anything to be sweet." She said quietly.

"You, my dear are wrong on that one. You seem sugary sweet and I do like you." I said to her.

Her face was flushed, she smiled this little side smirk and brushed her hair behind her ear. In that very moment time completely stopped. I was seeing this pictures float in front of my eyes. Like I was watching a film of someone's life. It was then I realized it was my own. Just not presently. It was odd to know I was seeing a life I didn't recognize. I saw her, it was Tatum but not. She did the same movement Tatum did as this flash back hit me. That must have triggered it inside of me. To see her like that again. I could see that we loved each other deeply, but I could also feel that I had done something to her that she wasn't even aware of that got her killed. I feel like my heart is being ripped out. I feel Tatum pull on my arm and it knocks the images away from my eyes.

"Are you okay?" She asked concerned.

"Yeah, I am. I mean I think so. Can I ask you something?" I said to her, fully prepared to sound crazy.

"Of course, what's wrong?" She said.

"What really happened to you when we were riding around town? Why did you scream like that?" I inquired, I needed to know because if my gut feeling is right then she saw the same thing that I did.

"Rhys I, I'm not sure I am comfortable sharing what happened. We just met and I don't think that we should be having this conversation right now." She said, her hands were shaking.

"Tatum, I understand what you are saying. I just need you to hear me, okay? It didn't just happen to you, I think it just happened to me too." I said, watching her face for a reaction.

"What?" That is the only word she said to me.

"I saw it too. I know what you know. Do you want to talk about it? We can grab our cups of coffee and go sit." I offered her, I reached out for her hand so she knew I was being genuine.

"Are you really suggesting we talk fate over coffee?" Tatum asked.

"I guess I am, yes." I replied.

She nodded and we walked over to her couch. We sat next to one another and we both started to share the things we saw. They were very similar. Not totally the same, which makes sense. We are two different people, we would surely see them prospectively different. She didn't know I had hurt her the way I did, so I told her about knowing she would die if we stayed together. Tatum began to cry. I felt like I was living in a book. This shit isn't something that happens to two ordinary people. I don't understand why we were even shown these things. We both felt now that we were totally connected to who we were in our last lives. In feeling that way, I knew I loved her already. I don't think I actually have any control over it.

"Tatum, I am so sorry for the things I did when I was someone else." I said to her.

"We aren't those people now, we are new. There is nothing to be sorry for." She said, leaning in to hug me.

I was grateful to have shared this experience with her. In truth, I understand why I did what I did previously. I would do anything to stay in her life. I now understand where the guilt came from that I felt when Tatum let out that scream. I let her die and hearing her in pain again was like living a nightmare. I wish I could say I would never do that to her again, but I am so drawn to her. Maybe sense we are both fully aware we can love in such a way that we get to live this time.

"What are you thinking, sweet girl?" I asked.

"Honestly?" She said back.

"Yes, honestly." I replied.

"I would like you to leave. I know we have this undeniable connection and apparently have all of these past lives together, but this karmic tie we share is toxic. I can't do this tonight. I'm sorry." She said as she walked toward her front door.

"I understand. I will go for the night. Sleep well, Tatum." I said as I left her home.

I heard the door close behind me. I was a bit angry, but that wasn't a fair emotion to feel. She was grieving herself and processing something huge. I don't blame her for needing space. I needed to accept the fact that I need to give that to her.

Number 5.

Tatum

I cannot stop sobbing. This stranger that I met at a bar is cosmically tied to me and is the reason I didn't live past my early twenties in a life I was never supposed to remember. I can say whole heartedly, this is such bullshit. When I said I like to carry myself as the main character of my own story, this is absolutely not what I had in mind. I hope my mom has some advice in the morning. I don't know how else I am going to get through this. She is the only one who will hold the answers that I need. My brain is on overload. My emotions are totally drained. I am grieving my last self. She didn't deserve to die like that. She didn't deserve such sadness and she didn't deserve to be loved by a boy who would let her die for his own personal feelings. What a cruel life I lived before. I am just grateful I didn't come back as fucked up in this life. I like this version of me. I do not want to risk her for the love of a boy who would kill me. I know I am supposed to know him, but that doesn't mean I need to die for him. That is unfair. I need to close my eyes. To forget all of this until morning. I can't allow myself to be this sad anymore.

I try and try to keep my eyes closed and to fall asleep. I just can't seem to shut my mind off. There is no way for me to not think about this random man I met at a bar who has now completely turned my world upside down. All I see when I shut my eyes are images of Olivia, of me. It keeps putting weight on my heart. I wish I had never had to remember the life I lived before. I don't like knowing I committed suicide. I hate knowing I let myself love someone so completely who all but let me die. I am hurting. I will carry this with me forever and I am not okay with that.

I pick up my phone and call my mom. The conversation starts with small talk and continues into me telling her about this mysterious boy from the bar last night. I could tell I didn't need to tell her much more. It was as if she already knew what I was going to say. She must have seen it too. That wouldn't be the first time we saw the same thing at the same time when it was related to a type of insane energy like this.

Her advice was simple. I needed to cut all ties with him. That this burden of death I carried in each life would continue again if I let myself care about him. I was blessed this time, I was given all the pieces so I could live. I was given a mother who could help guide me and keep me here. I won't let the stars win this time, they cannot have my life. My soul is mine to keep. I refuse to let this cycle continue.

I look over at the clock and realize it is already time for me to get ready for work. I need to shake last night off and pull myself together for this shift. I need to take a shower and put on a fresh face of makeup. Pick out a cute outfit and pack my book to read on break. I will have a good day, I will speak it into existence. I like my job, I stay busy pouring coffee for college students and professors. The distraction is absolutely welcomed.

I am off to work and am already feeling better. Knowing all of those things about my life and about Rhys doesn't mean I need to let it control my mood. I can either dwell on it and stay sad or accept the fact that last night happened and I have to push through the emotion of it all. Thankfully, I am quite good at pretending things didn't happen. I would get nothing done otherwise. I will make fun designs in the coffee foam at work and read my book when I can. Seizing my day, per usual.

That was a good thought anyway. As soon as I clock in at work I see Rhys sitting at one of the tables in the back. I never told him exactly where I work. I am not okay with him being here. The feeling of discomfort is so severe I start to feel sick. This is not normal behavior. Do I ask him to leave? Am I brave enough to even go over there to attempt to ask him that? I at least need to find out what he is doing here. One foot after the other I guess.

"Good morning. I didn't tell you where I work. What are you doing here?" I said to him, my voice was shaking.

"Oh hi Tatum, I honestly had no idea you worked here. I usually come by at open for a cup of coffee on my way into work but it is a Saturday and I have off so I came in later today." He said, I knew he was lying. He had a smirk on his face when I walked up to him. He was not surprised to see me.

"I got you, well I have to get back to work. Nice seeing you." I said shortly. I turned to walk away and he grabbed my arm.

"Excuse me, get your hands off of me." I yelled.

He dropped his hand and stood up. He made me so nervous. I didn't like the way he was behaving towards me. It was like a completely different person than the man I met last night.

"I didn't mean to offend you. It was just a natural reaction to get your attention as you turned away. You dropped your pen." He said sternly.

I did drop my pen, but that didn't make me feel any better about the situation. He didn't even apologize. He just continued to justify the things he was doing.

"You are fine, honest mistake. Next time just say my name, okay?" I replied. I knew I needed to keep a cool head, not only was I at work but I also did not want to give him the satisfaction.

He ran his fingers over the spot of my arm he had just grabbed, kissed my cheek and walked out of the shop. I couldn't shake how uneasy all of this felt. There has to be a reasonable explanation for his odd behavior this morning. I do not trust easily and meeting him last night felt utterly different from the version of him that was just in the coffee shop. I trusted my gut better than that and I would not have invited someone like that up to my apartment. If I see him again, I will come right out and ask what the hell all of that was about. I believe in second chances, but no more than two.

Number 6.

Rhys

I sat outside of the coffee shop for a few minutes after seeing her. I did not handle that well at all. I could tell I made her feel uneasy. I should not have come off so aggressively or that possessive. I have to figure out a way to explain all of this away. She has to believe I am not like that. That I wouldn't treat her that way. I can change for her. I would be whoever she needed me to be. All she has to do is tell me what she wants and it's hers. I love her and I need her to love me back. We are meant to be together. She has no choice in the matter. I didn't make the rules, for some reason the universe continues to bring new versions of us back to find one another. I have an obligation to the stars to love her. Tatum has that same obligation to love me in return. Free will went out the window when we met last night.

I need to go grab some groceries instead of sitting out here watching her. She wouldn't like this if she saw me. If I can come up with a good reason as to why I acted the way I did this morning, maybe she will let me make her dinner. Taking her out to is also an option. A public setting will make her more inclined to say yes after my stunt today.

Figuring out a reason to justify such unacceptable behavior is not an easy task to accomplish in a short period of time. The easiest approach would be to tell her it was because of our conversation last night. Feeding off of her emotions would work well I think. I could tell her I couldn't sleep and felt this sense of hostility over dying after watching her commit suicide. Have her feel a sense of guilt, we may be in different bodies now but we both know the truth.

I forgot to find out what time she gets off today. I will be romantic instead and bring flowers to her apartment and apologize to her for everything. Followed by an offer to take her out to dinner to make it up to her. There is a florist near my house that is outrageously expensive but the amount of exotic flowers I could present to her would be worth it. The effort needs to be clear, not subtle. I messed up this morning and I have to show her that the first impression she had of me was the right one.

This isn't normal behavior for me. I do not pursue women in this way, I have never felt the desire to. With Tatum though, I crave her. Every waking moment I am thinking about her, about the way she talks and about the way she smells. I want to spend all of my time just watching her read. She has no idea the hold she has over me. I want to tell her but I have already begun to come off too strong. Having that sort of premonition or vision into our past life has given me an in with her without even trying. She is cosmically tied to me.

I sat on the back of my bike for a moment to just imagine how last night would have gone if the universe didn't throw us a curve ball. Oh, sweet Tatum. Her hair is like fire, her eyes look like they were painted by the gods and the way her body moves is like Aphrodite herself taught her how to walk. I want to devour her. I have to win back her trust. I need her.

I am too anxious to grocery shop right now, I will just end up buying shit I don't need to pass the time. I am going to go back home, make a list and fuck around with my bike. It needs a good tune up anyway. I have to find something else to occupy the space in my mind that is not Tatum. I am starting to obsess. Attaching myself to her this deeply, this quickly is not something she would appreciate. I need to write myself reminders that this is not behavior she would approve of. I need to be making strategic moves to win her heart. She is so easy to read, I have studied her enough in the last forty or so hours to know what she will melt into and what will repel her. I need to come off less clingy, more go with the flow and absolutely, disgustingly romantic. Find words that will sound like porn to her ears. She is a reader, she loves the unrealistic love stories. Hell, we were practically handed that plot on a golden platter last night. All I have to do now is make sure she believes that I wouldn't hurt her this time around. If I can do that, then I get Tatum all to myself.

I am going to buy her flowers and a new outfit for myself to blow her away in. I will become everything she wants in a man and then some. I will show up to her place this evening with a well thought out apology and ask her to dinner. That is absolutely the plan. I have set it in motion. I know I can do this. I deserve to be the one who makes her smile. No one else can have that opportunity but me. I will win her back tonight. She slipped from me too fast. She is so strong willed. How do you break down a will like that? I do not understand how we can be fated to be together and yet I am still having to fight this hard for her.

I call the flower shop and place an order. I look up places to get a new outfit that is affordable and close to the flower shop so I can tackle all of that at once. I also need to figure out what time she gets off. I don't know how to do that without her knowing. I think the best plan of attack for that is going to be to get every errand done as fast as I possibly can and wait for her. I will need to find a place outside her building I can watch for her without her seeing me. I don't want her to know I was waiting. I need to be more casual when I approach her again.

I am going to jump in the shower to rinse off and get ready to leave the house for the rest of the day. As I am playing out this evenings scenarios in my head, I had a brilliant idea. If she does in fact invite me in instead of us going out to dinner, I can find a way to take a picture of her work schedule. That will help me know when I can make bold gestures. Tatum is so lucky to have someone like me try so hard for her in this way. I would do anything for her.

I throw on my outfit, not really caring what I look like because it is only temporary. Grab my keys and head out. I am ready to see her again. I can just picture her smiling at customers as she makes them their coffee. I envy every man who gets to look at her while she works today. I wish I hadn't acted the way I did this morning. I shouldn't have popped into her work before her shift. It was too obvious that I was there for her. I should have stopped in randomly not even acknowledging that she was there until I was about to walk out. I made a royal mistake that I will spend my entire day working to fix.

The bouquet of flowers I have ordered for her are astounding. They are huge, exotic flowers with greenery. Tons of eucalyptus to help destress the situation. I asked for more orange tones to the flowers to help match her home, I wanted her to see how much attention I paid to her space. I am impressed with this florist, they pulled off an astonishing arrangement of flowers that will without a doubt impress her by themselves. I just need to go find something nicer to wear, I want to match that dark academia vibe she gives off. Make her more attracted to me. I think a neutral toned button up, rolled straight leg pants and boots will do the trick. Tatum won't be able to resist a man dressed for her with the flowers I am presenting to her.

Now to rehearse exactly what I am going to say to her. I am thinking something along the lines of, "Tatum I am so sorry for the way I behaved in the coffee shop this morning, I wasn't myself. I was reeling over the conversation we had last night and the realization that I died because I couldn't handle the trauma you caused by committing suicide in my arms. I was struggling to accept that and also be okay with being tied to someone I don't know. You are beautiful and I would be the luckiest man in the world to know you. I wanted to come by to say that. I needed you to know that this apology came from the deepest parts of my heart. I would never do anything to hurt you. If you can find it in your heart to forgive me, I would like to take you to dinner this evening."

That will surely win her back, how could she possibly say no to such sweet words? I am finally outside her place. The good news is I don't have to wait out here long. Tatum is already home. I can see her through her window. She is changing out of her work clothes. I want to see her this way up close. I don't want to watch her naked body through a window, yet I can't look away. She looks as if she was sculpted. Each curve perfectly placed. I was beginning to crave her again. I need to snap out of this daze and go up to her. It's time to get my woman back.

Number 7.

Tatum

I am finally off work and able to get comfortable. I love taking off clothes and shoes after a long shift and sliding into something silk lined. I want to read and totally shut my mind off. This morning did not start off good, last night was a travesty and I just need to really forget any of it even happened. A shower, or maybe a hot bath should help. Then silk pajamas and a good book. I will make some coffee and add ninety percent cream. I am already finding peace in knowing how my evening is going to go.

I undress and start brewing some coffee. I don't want it too hot when I am ready for it so I figured if I start it before my shower it will be perfect when it is time to sit down and relax. I walk into the bathroom to start the water and as soon as my hand grabs the handle there is a knock at the front door. I didn't invite anyone over and I hardly ever get random visitors. Anyone who knows me knows to text me beforehand. I grab my robe off of the back of the bathroom door and tie it around my waist.

I look through the peep hole and it's Rhys. I honestly don't know if I want to open the door or not. I guess it would be rude not to. Here goes nothing I suppose.

"Hi Rhys." I say as I open the door.

"Tatum, hi." He said smiling at me.

"What are you doing here?" I asked.

"I am so sorry for my behavior earlier, Tatum. It was unacceptable. I was reeling from the conversation we had last night and the realization that I died because I couldn't deal with the trauma of you committing suicide in my arms. That's a really difficult thing to process and I know you get that. I also needed to figure out how to be okay with being tied to someone I hardly know. You are beautiful and it would be the pleasure of my life to know you. I wanted to come by to apologize to you. It is the very least I could do. If you can find it in your heart to forgive me, I would really like to take you to dinner, and also give you these flowers." He said to me. He seems so genuine.

I am honestly so taken back right now. I don't even know what to say or do. He is right, I do understand. I have been having a tough time with all of it myself. He is very sweet, maybe I should forgive him. I mean what harm could dinner do, right?

"Thank you for coming all the way over here to apologize to me. I really do appreciate it. The flowers are just so beautiful. Thank you." I said, trying my best to find the right words.

"Of course, and if you aren't in the mood to go out to dinner that is one hundred percent okay." Rhys replied.

"You know what, yes. We can go to dinner. Have a do over of last night. Hopefully not have any more life altering epiphanies while we are out." I said jokingly.

"Let's hope not." He answered laughing at me.

"Why don't you come in while I shower and get ready? You can help yourself to some coffee and I will get you the remote." I offered.

"Sounds perfect. Think of where you would like me to take you tonight while you shower." He smiled.

I made sure he was comfortable and I walked back into the bathroom. I don't know if I made the right call. Dinner really isn't a dangerous endeavor though. We have already gone through the worst of it as far as first encounters go. I think talking through it may be the right thing for us to do. We are both clearly having a hard time processing everything we know about our pasts. Maybe the best thing is for us to lean on one another right now.

I take the quickest shower and put my robe back on. I need to put on makeup and blow dry my hair. Then I will walk out and decide what I am going to wear. I know we have loved each other before but that doesn't mean I am not going to put the effort in this time around. I throw a towel in my hair and start putting foundation on. I crack the door to let some steam out and also to peak at Rhys. He is just sitting on my couch. He put the flowers in a vase which is such a small but sweet gesture. He really is so attractive. His dark hair and light skin is such a pretty combination. His choice of outfit today helped him a lot too. It wasn't as frat boy casual, it was clean and put together. I liked it a lot. He was impressive, I couldn't deny it.

I finished my makeup and my hair was as dry as I could get it without damaging it. I walk out of the bathroom and we immediately make eye contact. He smiled at me so gently, it was comforting. I went over to my closet and grabbed my favorite plaid pants and a sweater. It was simple but still very cute. Of course I had to add the gold jewelry and black boots, it's my thing. I walk back around to be in his view and I got surprisingly bold.

"How do I look?" I asked Rhys. I even did a half twirl. I am such an embarrassing creature.

"You, my sweet Tatum look absolutely ravishing." He said to me.

My heart fluttered. What words, unexpected ones at that.

"Why thank you, sir. I appreciate your kindness." I said, giggling as I went to walk away.

I was officially excited for this date. I know in my heart I shouldn't be and that I cannot let myself fall for him but damn it, this is not easy. We really are pulled together in such a magnetic, other worldly way. It's odd, but in a wonderful way.

"Are you ready to go?" I yelled from the bathroom.

"Whenever you are." He replied.

"I am just about ready to walk out the door. I have no idea where I want to go for dinner. Can you just surprise me?" I asked.

"Absolutely. I have a great idea. I also brought you an extra helmet this time. Safety first." He said to me.

God, he is so cute. We walk out the door and out to his motorcycle. I can't lie, I love that this is his only form of transportation. It makes me have to do something outside of my comfort zone. We slide on and start off down the road. We aren't stopping anywhere in town, so I have no clue where we are going. To be fair, that is what I asked him to do. The further from campus we get the more I begin to realize where he is taking me. We are going to his place. My entire body tenses up and is ignited with energy I do not like. We were supposed to go out to dinner, not go to his home to eat. There is nothing that I can do at this point except go with it.

I take a huge deep breath as we pull in his driveway. He steps off his bike and held out his hand.

"I hope you don't mind, I thought it would be nice to order in, this way you are still out of your house. It is just quieter here, we can actually talk." He said to me.

"Yeah, this is fine." I said as I got off his bike.

I set the helmet down and proceed with the utmost caution. This is exactly the situation I needed to avoid with him. It isn't even that I am uncomfortable being at his house, it's that I am now in a vulnerable situation with a man that I am somehow fated to be with. I have no control over anything that happens here.

I follow him inside and try to get myself to stop shaking. This is one date, I have nothing to be afraid of. Fate doesn't work this fast, we don't even know how we feel about one another. Meant to be or not we have had less than a hand full of conversations. I cannot let my anxiety take over right now. I need to be present and clear headed. Everything will be okay. He is sweet and handsome, well-spoken and apologetic. He wouldn't do something to make me uncomfortable. If that were the case he would not have went out of his way to say sorry the way that he did. I can't be afraid of all of the unknowns surrounding us. Rhys and I will figure this out. Together.

Number 8.

Rhys

Tatum is in my house. The feelings I have are overwhelming. I am so grateful she has forgiven me, but now the pressure is on to be the perfect guy for her. I need to make her feel secure in this space, like she can relax and open up. I can tell she is distancing herself. She has expressed her battle with who we are to one another so I am sure that is what is wrong. I will open up to her first, let the flood gates burst.

"I know this isn't exactly what I promised you for tonight, and I can tell it is a little off putting. I just feel like we really need to talk about what happened yesterday and I am not sure a public setting is the best place for that." I said to her.

"You are right, I understand now. I don't know that I would have been comfortable opening up with people sitting all around that could hear us." Tatum said.

That is what I needed to hear. We are getting somewhere now.

"Why don't you get comfortable, I will order us some food and you can just relax." I offered.

"That actually sounds wonderful," She said, letting out a big sigh.

I was unaware that I could love a sound that someone made so much. I began to wonder what other sounds Tatum made that I would love. I need to tuck that thought away for when she is not around. I need to pick us out somewhere to order from. Pizza is always a safe bet. I will get that with side salads and garlic bread. That way there are options for her to choose from. I pop my head around the corner of the kitchen to see how she is doing. I am so mesmerized by her. Instead of sitting and relaxing, she is running her fingers over my movie collection and slowly reading each title. She really loves the details of the simple things. I could watch her just simply exist for the rest of my days. I just have to convince her to want that as well.

The food will be here shortly. I need to clear off the kitchen table and pour us a drink. I hope she is at least kind of enjoying her night. I want her to become comfortable around me and this is the place I am most myself, therefore giving me the upper hand as far as making her want me. I can tell Tatum is interested. She won't allow herself to fall for me because she is too afraid of the things we have control over. The only thing I can do is try my very best tonight to show her that she has nothing to be worried about.

"Tatum, would you like wine or water with dinner?" I asked.

"Actually, I will have both if you don't mind." She answered.

I nodded and went to pour her drinks. She followed me back into the kitchen. Tatum pressed her body up against the island in the middle of the kitchen and was just watching me grab the glasses and wine out of the fridge. She was actually making me nervous. I have never noticed a woman watching me before. It is quite literally always the other way around.

"So what did you order us for dinner?" She asked.

"I ordered us pizza with side salads and garlic knots. I figured it was a good option and if I am being truthful, pizza is my go to comfort food." I said to her.

"That actually sounds so amazing right now. You definitely made the right call." She said back to me.

"Good, it should be here any minute now. I am about done setting the table so as soon as it arrives we can eat. If it would make you more comfortable, after we are done we can go somewhere else. Back to your place or just get another drink in town." I offered.

"Let's play it by ear. You never know how a night can play out." Tatum said, with the most beautiful smile on her face.

I agreed and before I could come up with something else to say there was a knock at the door.

"Food is here." I said to her.

I walked outside and grabbed the food. I set it down on the dining room table and called out for her to come join me. I opened everything up for us to just make our plates. She grabbed three slices of pizza, a few garlic knots and her salad. That is my kind of girl, she isn't embarrassed to eat when she is hungry. That is a quality I like in a woman, unapologetically herself in all things. Not just her brain and her looks. She does not care what the world around her thinks and I think that is something to admire.

"You really were hungry weren't you?" I asked, laughing.

"I told you I was ready to eat." Tatum replied, laughing even with food in her mouth.

I just laughed along with her. We just sat and shared the silence as we ate. It was refreshing, to not feel the pressure of a typical first date. She seems much more relaxed now. I wanted to strike up a conversation but I wasn't sure where to start. I had so much I needed to convince her of. I don't know which one of those things should take precedence. Tatum wanted to talk about everything from the night before. I will have to do my best to tie it all together.

"Tatum, I want to talk about the things we saw last night. How we are bound together and how you are feeling about it all." I said to her, I reached for her hand so she knew I did truly want to know what she had to say.

"I am overwhelmed by it all if I am being totally honest. To meet a handsome stranger who winds up being the man you have loved sense time itself began is more than intense. Especially being hit with large floods of images of us in our last life together, I died. You died, too young. I am not sure what to do with all of that." She answered. She looked so sad.

"I am feeling the same way. I haven't been able to accept all of it. I can't write it off and move past it. The fact of the matter is we are made for each other. We have lived over twenty years on this planet with our entire futures together planned out without us knowing. That's insane." I said to her.

I was overcome with the smell of lavender and rosemary. It was so out of nowhere and I know Tatum wasn't wearing that scent. It is strange, but it is a comforting smell. It changed my mood. Like I was all of the sudden the calmest I have ever been.

"I know it is insane." Tatum said. "I don't necessarily like the idea of my life being fated to a man I don't know. I don't like that I killed myself. I don't like that a version of myself hurt so deeply. I don't like that I hurt you in that way. That is so unbelievably unfair. I am so sorry I did that to you. I am sorry to myself for not being strong enough to fight." She continued.

"Please don't apologize for parts of our souls that are gone. We are not them anymore. We don't live there anymore. We are here, right now. You are not Olivia. You are Tatum and you built yourself stronger than she was. This version of you is so powerful." I told her, staring her right in her eyes.

She reached for my hand with tears pouring from her gentle, beautiful eyes. I lifted my hand to wipe her tears away. I wanted to hold her but I didn't want to push it right now. She needed subtle comfort and a way to vent about the weight shared between us.

"Thank you Rhys. I need you to know I do forgive you for this morning, I know how crazy this thing is between us. I don't blame you for acting out of character. You are so kind. I am so glad you came by tonight. Talking about all of this with you makes me feel like we are really going to get through this together." She said, running her fingers over the side of my hand.

I did it. I got her right where I need her to be. I feel free to say things now. I captured her heart. I actually pulled this off.

"Tatum I am so thankful you forgive me. I don't want to lose you. Not now, not ever. I know that our lives have been bound by death and heartache for all of time but I promise you I will not allow that to happen this time. We were given an extraordinary gift, we know everything this time. The both of us. We can fight fate together." I poured my heart at her feet.

She gave me a sweet, small smile and leaned into my chest. I knew she loved me too. We didn't even have to say the words. It was a shared emotion embedded in our souls before we were even brought back to life. You cannot deny the connection we share. Free will is gone, we belong to one another. I would not have it any other way.

I lifted her chin to make her look up at me. I placed my hand on her cheek and the other hand on the side of her neck. I pulled her into me and kissed her. We melted into each other like only Shakespeare could write about. I felt her breathing against my chest. Her lips were soft, like rose petals. I love the way she smells, the closer she is to me the more I realize I was wrong. She is the smells of lavender and the hints of rosemary. She is intoxicating. She pulled back from me.

"Rhys, there is no guarantee we can fight the fact that if we love each other we will die, or at the very least I will. I cannot deny that we are meant to be together. For tonight, I am willing to forget about all of it. To forget that kissing you is like signing my own death certificate. I can't promise you what we will be in the morning. For now though, I am yours." She whispered.

I wasn't exactly happy she was still having trouble believing we can be together and live happily but I wanted her. As she said, for tonight she is mine and I will have her. I leaned back into her and kissed her deep. I wanted our breathing to coincide with one another. Fuck, I love her.

She let herself move from her chair and into my lap. She was grinding her body against mine, I ran my hands down her back and traced her spine. How can she deny me the love I know we both share? Each bone in her body belonged to me. I want to enjoy this intimate time with her but all I can think about is how I am going to get her to stay when morning comes. I need a plan. She kissed my neck and I could feel her form a smile as she kissed further down my body. We will see where this goes first so my head is in the game. Then I will find a way to keep her in my grasp.

I picked her up and held her by the middle of her thighs. I walked us into my room and laid her down slowly onto the bed. I hope my bed sheets smell like her forever. She starts taking her clothes off and as soon as my eyes can see every beautiful inch of her ivory skin I could feel time slow down. The world was moving in a motion that was not real. I went to close my eyes to kiss her again and I froze. All of the sudden I no longer saw Tatum. It was Olivia. She was sitting on my bed staring at me. I jumped back and had no words. What do I say? I don't even know if this is real. She is shaking her head back and forth, mouthing the word no. I reach my hand out to touch her and she feels like ice. I felt her, she was dead. She has been gone, I don't understand what is going on. Olivia stood up in front of me and leaned in to say something in my ear. It was such a hushed sound. I couldn't make it all out.

"Rhys, don't you dare touch her. We know who you are. We see the way you look at us, she is me and I am her. I feel everything you are doing. Your kiss and your viper tongue have no power over Tatum. She is stronger than I was. She will see both of your faces and she will fight you to the death." Olivia said as she faded away.

I feel like I am going to pass out. I don't know what is real anymore. I feel like time is slipping through me and not around me. My vision is fading.

Number 9.

Tatum

Rhys went in to kiss me and then hit the ground, I am over top of him trying to get him to come to and he isn't moving. He is breathing but he isn't responding to me. I run into his bathroom and grab a cup of water to splash on his face.

"Rhys I need you to open your eyes for me, okay?" I keep saying over and over again hoping he will hear me.

He started making a grunting sound and I can see his eyes moving from behind his eye lids. If he is making movements I am going to throw this cold water on to his face and hope he opens his eyes. The water hit his skin and it was like it created an electric current that pulsed through him to jolt him awake. He say straight up and looked at me.

"What happened?" He asked me.

"I am not sure, we were getting a little hot and heavy and you went in to kiss me and then passed out. Are you okay?" I questioned.

"I think so, yeah. I am sorry if I scared you. I didn't even feel like life was real. I saw you but it wasn't you. I don't know how to explain it. I'm fine." Rhys said.

"I think you should go ahead and lay down. I will grab you a towel to dry your face and then you should get into bed." I said.

I helped him into bed and went to grab him a towel. I don't know what happened back there, but a big part of me was glad it did. I let myself get carried away in the moment with him, I couldn't help it. I had no self-control. Weather I like it or not a part of me loves him. I don't have a choice in the matter. I do know I can't be with him. I need to distance myself and not allow this imprinted instinct in me to take over. My life depends on it.

I help him dry off and bring him a fresh glass of water to sit on his bedside table. I want to make sure he is one hundred percent alright before I go. I have a feeling he is going to try to convince me to stay, I have to fight him. I will remain kind because we are like one person, but I can't let myself stay the night here. I don't want to feel anything more for him. I hope he can understand that. I won't have that conversation with him tonight, he needs to not stress and rest after passing out like that.

"If you are comfortable and all set I am going to get a ride home. You need to sleep and I have to work a short shift in the morning and get some homework done." I said.

He looked sad but also looked so exhausted that he didn't have the energy to care. Which I was thankful for. I didn't want to have to keep telling him I was leaving no matter what he said. I kissed him on the forehead and booked a ride home. I sat on the edge of his bed and rubbed his head as he fell asleep. I am so full of love for him in this moment. He is so at peace, so vulnerable and it is kind of beautiful. To see him so unguarded. I wonder what he is dreaming about. I can see his eyes fluttering around behind the lid. He is breathing kind of heavy. Maybe I will send him a text in the morning and ask about it. Right now though, it is time for me to go.

I collect all of my things and walk out of his house. I step into the car and take a long, deep breathe. I hate feeling so out of control. I plan things in my life out so well so I have no fear of the future. I still do things spontaneously just not drastically. What is happening in our lives right now is not something I would have ever predicted. I am far too ordinary to be fated to be anything to anyone. Let alone be a part of something cosmic that I couldn't even begin to understand. Most of all, I hate that no matter how many times I tell myself that I can't care about him, not intensely or deeply anyway, my heart screams at me. I love him. I don't even know him, but I do. It doesn't logically make any god damn sense.

I am at a loss. I have already gone to my mother for advice. She told me to run. Get out and far away from all of this. I want to do that but that is not possible.

In our moments of madness I have laid down roots. I am intertwined with him. This is of no volition of mine. I am hopeless, and I am terrified. If I allow this ivy to grow so tall that it cannot be cut down, I will surely come face to face with the devil. The scariest part of it all is not that I love him without authority, but that when I meet the devil I will know his face. It will be his.

My intuition is strong, my faith is stronger. I know better than to let myself love him. My death resides in his eyes. I make this mistake every time I am brought back to life. Why is this battle so hard to fight? I am here, sword in hand ready to cut the ties that bind us. It is in the very moment I go to break this chord that I freeze and turn back. I need to find a way to not let the stars or Rhys have such a strong hold on me. This is the most dangerous encounter I will ever come face to face with.

I am finally home and step inside my door. I get comfortable and throw my curls up into a messy bun. I go to the bathroom to look at myself in the mirror. I need to say something out loud and it is directed at me.

"You are stronger than this. You know you will die if you love him. You know you want to live. Do not let fate trick you into believing you owe it something, because you don't."

As I am saying this I see the image of myself begin to blur in the mirror and a flash of women take my place, the last one being Olivia. If I am right, I am seeing every lost version of my soul. Every broken woman who died loving him. I feel fragmented. Every ounce of pain I have carried through these lives is brought swiftly to the surface. I am staring into the eyes of Olivia, I reach my hand out to touch the reflection in the mirror. She is reaching back, meeting her hand sent shivers down my spine. A shot of lightening has gone through my fingers and down to my feet. They all came forth out of the furthest parts of the vastness of my soul to give me the strength to beat fate this time.

I now carry the strength of every woman I have ever been.

Number 10.

Rhys

Waking up this morning was dreadful. Whatever happened to me last night with Tatum and Olivia has drained me. I feel like a walking corpse. I guess that analogy isn't an appropriate one, but it is how I feel. I need to get out of bed and eat something. At the very least I need to knock back some water and check my phone. I want to text Tatum and apologize for passing out on her in the middle of our moment. I can't imagine how mortified she must have been. Actually, I can because I am on the other end of that feeling.

I pick up the cup of water off of the nightstand and my phone. I don't have any messages from her. I wish she would have at least told me that she made it home safely. She is so independent, but she has someone who cares about her now. I need to know she is okay. I will let it slide for the simple fact that she had to leave my house last night instead of spending it in my bed because I couldn't keep my shit together.

After I finish this glass I am going to get in the shower. I need to rinse last night off. Feeling refreshed will help me muster up the power to send her a message and ask her to see me today so I can tell her what actually happened last night. The only issue is that I still do not fully understand what went down last night. Tatum made it sound like I immediately passed out, which would mean it was all happening in my head when I fell and not actually happening right in front of me. I guess that makes the most sense, it felt more real than that though. Almost as if Olivia had clawed her way to the surface of Tatum to tell me to leave her be. Either way, her warning is irrelevant. Olivia may be a part of Tatum but they are not the same. I refuse to let some ghost from our past scare me away from the love we share. I am not Wren either. I need to remember that. I am not so weak that I would kill myself because a woman I love died in my arms, I would have been strong enough to keep her alive. I do understand his choices in a way, I can't live without Tatum either. I pay enough attention to her though to be able to stop her from hurting herself if that problem were to arise.

Stepping out of the shower, I feel so much better. I have brushed off last night's odd encounter with my past and am moving forward with my day. I won't just show up at Tatum's job again, I learned that lesson. She also mentioned having to do homework. Maybe I will stop by while she is home later to talk to her and apologize for not doing my job as a man last night.

As I am planning out my day my phone started to buzz. I have a message from Tatum. My fingers could not open this message fast enough. It said- "I hope you are feeling better this morning. I was hoping later in the day you and I could find some time to sit down and talk. Let me know. XO, Tatum."

That sounded promising. She signed it with kisses. Of course I am going to go see her later. I replied to her and am just going to wait for her to tell me place and time. I have nothing else to do today but wait to see her. I will probably clean up the bike while I wait but other than that, I will just anticipate the conversation she wants to have with me. I love that she checked on me first. Of course she would though, that's just how she is. She has such a caring, gentle nature. It is one of the many reasons why I love her.

Tatum sent another message telling me to meet her at the coffee shop she works at when her shift is over this afternoon. Her first message to me this morning seemed sweet and I believed it was going to be a good conversation. Now I am not so sure. She doesn't want to have this talk at her place, she chose a public setting. Which is the thing to do if you are going to be telling someone something you know will make them unhappy. It helps avoid confrontation. That may be true but she does not know me the way she would like to think she does. I will not allow her to slip through my fingers. I am unsure how I can make that anymore clear to her.

Number 11.

Tatum

I feel confident today, in everything. In my ability to tell Rhys we cannot know each other any longer. If there is any hope of survival, today needs to be the last conversation we have. I am concerned with how he will react to this news, so I decided to tell him this when I get off work with people all around. He will be here soon, and my heart is heavy. I know that this is the only way to save our lives but I still feel the stitches that bind our skin together so tightly.

Last night showed me that it does not matter what I feel for him. I have chosen him in every life and have not lived long enough to actually say I lived. I deserve more than that. I can't let myself care if I break his heart. This is the best decision for us both. It is the safest course of action.

While I am clocking out I hear the rumble of his motorcycle as he pulls up in front of the shop. I am less nervous than I thought I would be. I am ready to end this brief but tragically painful part of my life. He walks in the door and smiles at me. I wave and give myself a second to harness the power I know is sitting right beneath the surface. I have to do this.

"Hey beautiful." He said as he wrapped his arms around me.

"Hi Rhys. Come sit with me for a minute. Can I get you a coffee?" I offered, my hands were shaking a bit.

"No, I am okay. Thank you though. What is it that you needed to talk about?" He asked me. I can tell he knows this isn't going to play out the way he would like it to.

"Look, I care about you. A lot. I have enjoyed talking to you and I know that we are supposed to be together. I know that we have chosen one another every single time, over and over again without fail. Though a love story filled with such brokenness may be viewed as beautiful, I don't think I can choose you this time." I said, fumbling with my hands.

"I think you are wrong. I think you want to choose me this time, you just won't let yourself because you aren't brave enough." He said angrily.

"Excuse me? I am more than brave enough, in fact I think what I am doing by telling you I am walking away from this is quite brave." I replied sternly.

"I disagree. You want this. You don't have a choice in the matter. I think you know that, too." His face is turning red.

I am now filled with so much resentment and anger I refuse to be kind about this anymore. I will not allow him to speak to me this way. No matter how upset he is, he will not talk down to me. Disrespect is not something I take lightly.

"Do you want to know what I think? I think you are selfish. I think you are arrogant and spiteful. You are acting like a child." I began to yell.

"Is that so? If you believe all of those things of me then why do you love me?" Rhys said.

I cannot even begin to fathom how there is love for him in my heart. He is not the man I have been around for the last two days. This is a version of him I feel more hatred for than any form of love. I am no longer sorry for hurting him.

"That's just it. I do love you, despite all of those things. You are right in one thing only, I can't control loving you. It is not my choice. What is my choice, is choosing myself instead of you. I cannot allow myself to love a man who would let me die as a condition to a temporary love with me. I want to live this life fully and unapologetically. I won't have that chance if I pick you. Therefore, I am not. You and I will be nothing to each other from here on out." I am screaming at him now.

He says absolutely nothing. He looks so angry, but he won't speak. He stands up and my heart begins to pound. If this conversation has shown me anything it is that I never knew him. This man is not like the ones I have chosen before. For some reason this version of his soul is tainted with something dark. I made the right choice. He is just staring at me now. He turns away from me and walks out of the coffee shop and gets on his bike. His tires squeal as he pulls away. I am overcome with such relief I begin to cry. I feel free.

I went into today thinking that battling our fate was going to be a true fight, that it would break me and I would be so sad. Instead, I came out stronger than I could have ever imagined. Having to say all of those things to Rhys awakened an evil inside of him I had yet to see. This is why Olivia came forward last night, she could feel something was not right and that I needed some guidance to be able to open my eyes to it.

The only thing I have left to worry about now is if he will truly stay away. He said nothing after my outburst. His silence concerned me more than his anger, because I have no idea what he was thinking. I know there is still good in him. I have come face to face with all of my souls, accepting them and each decision they made in choosing him. He has not. The energy he is feeling is being shoved down and out, he isn't processing it. Until he does, I am afraid he will spiral. Maybe I should have tried to help him before I told him to never speak to me again. I am far too kind for my own good, I am always trying to save people. I need to realize that saving myself today was the absolute right thing to do and there was no waiting on it.

Number 12.

Rhys

Tatum just made a huge mistake. Did she honestly think that was going to work? Showing me how cruel she could be? I warned her I would not be so easily deterred and that she will be mine. I told her she had no choice. Thinking she won and is free of us is just ignorant.

In my anger I start throwing things around my living room, in doing so I noticed something I had forgotten about. Something that is going to play a huge part in getting her back. Tatum's work schedule. I took a picture of it when she was getting ready the other night and printed a copy. Devising a plan will be much easier with this information at hand.

Keeping Tatum's heart in my hands will consist of one very important piece, convincing her she will not die because of me. That I am not Wren, that I will protect her and that she can love me freely without worry. That's when it hit me. The perfect way to show her I would save her.

I head straight to my computer, her work schedule in hand. It is time to lay out this plan. The first step is to find someone willing to be paid to scare her. I am sure there are websites for things like this. There has to be some creep out there who gets off on making women afraid without physically harming them, why else would people want to work at haunted houses? My thought process is, I hire someone to pretend to mug her when she gets off of work one day in the evening. I swoop in at just the right time and save her. Then, in her traumatized mind set I can convince her that in my presence she did not die, but she was saved. Then she can let her guard down and choose me. I know her heart wants to, she just needs a little nudge. This plan is bulletproof. It is genius.

Looking over her schedule she only works two evening shifts over the course of the next two weeks. I think it would be best to choose the second evening shift, that way there is no suspicions that it could be my doing. I need to be smart about this. There is absolutely no room for mistakes. It has to be one hundred percent authentic.

Tatum needs to believe she was in the wrong place at the wrong time and that I just so happened to be in the right one. I know she locks up at the side door, which is perfect because there will be less foot traffic. This random man will come up from behind her and hold a knife to her stomach. He will demand her purse and the keys to the coffee shop and then I will come in and save her. She will look at me with a hero complex and will just have to allow herself to believe she can be with me.

I stumble upon this dark website that is just disgusting. It is exactly what I have been looking for. I need to make a post on what I need from someone and hope I get a bite. I don't think it will be too hard to find someone to do this, looking through this site it is abundantly clear to me that I do not know the people of this city in the slightest. While I wait for a response I write out the plan detail by detail. I circle the date and add in the time of the attack to her work schedule. This will be laid out so well that there will be no way to slip up.

I have already gotten three emails about my post. Two of these men seem too intense to even consider. I don't want to be worried that Tatum could potentially be in real danger. I need to know going into this that this man is only in it for the scare. The other email I have received seems to fit the bill pretty well. I reply to his offer and I think he will accept. I am offering three hundred dollars for his services. In retrospect that seems a little steep but I need him to take this job seriously. He can't fuck up, one wrong step and she could figure it out. Or this man could get arrested and rat me out. Every other scenario but success is not a good one.

I wonder what Tatum is doing right now. I hate the way we left things. I shouldn't have just walked away. I could tell it wasn't the time to try to fight for her though. She was fuming, I pushed her to her limit. I needed to back down. Who knows how things would have gone if I hadn't left when I did. Surely I would not have thought of this plan to have her safely back in my arms. Fate is on my side. It has been all along. She has to be with me. There is no way to cheat the system we were created for. This has been our duty to the universe time and time again. I have accepted that. She needs to as well.

I wouldn't be having to go through all of this trouble if she wasn't so strong willed and could just accept that she has to do this. Tatum made this decision whether she remembers it or not, she chose to give her life when time began. She can't just act as if there isn't a continuous debt to be paid. Instead of running away, she should just love me until the time comes around again that we pay our price.

No matter, I have a plan. I have the backing of the cosmos. She won't get away this time.

Number 13.

Tatum

This last week has been nothing but light. I feel so free of worry. Rhys hasn't tried to contact me at all and I haven't seen him around. I think I really did it. Between work and school and no unexpected surprises, I have still found the time to really relax, to enjoy the smaller moments. I was always a minimalist, except when it comes to my messy collection of books. When you are faced with a fate like death over loving someone, you start to appreciate more things in life. I never noticed how the owner of my favorite book store in town had her husband come by every night to help her with closing, they danced in the dim light of the shop yesterday. It was beautiful. I would have never noticed that and stopped to appreciate someone else's life without this experience. I am so grateful.

I am also overcome with heartache. Olivia, well I, never got to experience the true beauty life had to offer. She couldn't fight it anymore. I hate how badly life treated us before. Her mind was such a dangerous place to live. Wren didn't help her, I know she loved him and was blinded by the intense love they shared. I just wish she could have pushed through. At least I know now that I deserve more than a love that would consume me to the point of death. There is more to me than emotions. I am more than a woman made to be a lover or a wife. I am strong and independent, smart and kind. I will do great things in this life. I can't risk that for the love of a man.

I take the idea from the bookstore clerk across the way and dim the lights to the coffee shop while I close up tonight. I turn the music up a bit louder than normal and allow myself to feel some peace. To live inside my own little world. It is well deserved as of late. I pick up the mop and start singing into the top of it like a microphone. I feel like a kid again, so fearless. This is good for me. I dance around the empty shop as I pick up the chairs and set them on top of the tables. I should make this what I do every time I am the only one left at work. I would be doing myself such a favor ending my shifts this way. It is as if a rush of serotonin runs through every vein in my body and sets fireworks off in my brain. I hope to feel this way longer than this one moment in time. This is what I had been fighting for.

I am almost done with the checklist for closing when I feel this strong wave of energy come over me. It is similar to the way I felt last week when I came face to face with every version of myself. Something inside of me told me to walk into the bathroom to look in the mirror again, so I do. I flip the light switch on and instead of seeing myself in the reflection of the mirror I see Olivia. She reaches out for me again and I can hear her say something. It is so faint I can't make out the words. I can feel in bones she is warning me of something but without knowing what she is saying to me I will just take this and be cautious. I turn the light off and walk out to clock out and grab my things.

I walk around to double check everything and make sure the front door is bolted up. I hate using the side door to leave but it is the safest for the shop to have the front doors locked up from the inside, so I understand. It just isn't lit very well down the side of the building and tends to make me uneasy. I reach in my purse to grab my pocket sized tasor and realize I left it charging at home. What good is it going to do me sitting on the counter? There is nothing that

I can do about it now. I shake it off and walk out the door. As I am putting my keys into the lock I hear something behind me. At first it just sounded like the wind rustling the trash on the ground, but I am quickly starting to realize something is wrong. I see a shadow approach me from the side and feel hands grab me. I am spun around so fast I couldn't even scream and there is a large man in a black ski mask standing in front of me. I feel something pressed against my stomach. It's a knife. I am completely frozen in fear. He puts his other arm forcefully against my throat.

"Give me your purse and the keys to the store." He yells at me, spit flying in my face.

"You can take whatever you'd like sir, just please don't hurt me." I don't even know if that was the right thing to say but I have never prepared myself for a situation like this.

He grabbed my bag out of my hand and threw it on the ground to put his arm back up against my throat. I was shaking so hard, I couldn't breathe. I don't know what to do. He has my purse and my keys and is still not letting me go. If this is fates way of fucking me I am not okay with it.

I can smell cigarettes and booze seeping from his breath as he comes in closer to me. He pushes himself into me and I start to prepare for the worst. I would rather him kill me than do what I think he is about to. I hear a voice shouting off to the left of me. Thank god someone saw us. Maybe I make it out of this alive. Everything feels like a blur. I am not even sure how far away this other person is from helping me. Close enough to scare my attacker off. He let me go, his arms are no longer on my body and my stomach is free of the knife that started pressing into my stomach.

"Tatum are you okay?" I heard the voice say.

I look up from the ground and it's Rhys. He saved my life. How is this even possible? We were shown that to be near one another is to die. I don't care right now, I am just grateful he walked by when he did.

"Rhys thank you." That is all I could get myself to say to him.

I fell into his arms and cried. He held me for a moment and then moved me backward.

"You are bleeding. Did he hurt you?" Rhys is starting to panic.

I didn't even notice that I was bleeding. I was in such shock I guess I didn't feel like knife actually do any damage.

"I'm alright, I don't even feel it." I whispered.

"I hear you but we need to get you to a hospital. You need to get looked at. We need to call the police." He is rambling.

I don't even care to call the police. He is gone, I am okay. It's over. The right thing to do would be to allow the authorities to look for him so no one else gets hurt. I just don't want to relive it after it just happened.

"You can call them. I am going to sit against the wall." I said.

He grabbed his phone out of his pocket and called for an ambulance and an officer. I don't even want to look at my stomach. I don't want to see it, I know I will get sick if I do. I already feel nauseous. This doesn't happen around here. There is always security driving around. I may be a nervous bird but I was never afraid for my life like that before.

After I sat down, things moved really fast around me. They were hounding me with questions as the EMT's checked my wound, they were taping off the area and interviewing Rhys. I have to go to the hospital for stitches, they say it isn't deep and that I got lucky. I don't feel lucky. I feel like the universe has targeted me. I started to fight their plans for me and this is what happens. Oddly enough though, Rhys is the one who saved me. He wasn't the cause of my death but the reason I got to walk out of that traumatic experience with my life. I find myself wanting to kiss him. To really thank him for saving me. For him to forgive me for the way I acted last week. I need him to understand I am only trying to save us both. For now though, I need to make sure he knows how thankful I am. He rescued me, I am in one entire piece because of him. I don't know what this means for us, quite frankly it doesn't matter right now.

After the police are done questioning me, I am sent off in the ambulance and Rhys jumps in with me. I reach for his hand and whole it so tight.

"Thank you for saving my life. I don't know what he would have done to me if you hadn't come by when you did." I said, holding back tears.

He started to brush the hair out of my face and put his hand on my cheek.

"Please don't thank me. I don't know what I would have done if anything had happened to you Tatum. I love you." He said.

I couldn't hold back the tears anymore. I was in so much pain and so shaken, to have him next to me telling me he loves me is such a gift.

"And I love you." I replied.

Number 14.

Rhys

I did it. I was her hero. I am holding her in an ambulance and she loves me. Nothing could ruin this moment for me, for us. Except for the fact that he hurt her. Tatum has to go get stitches, I paid him to not lay a finger on her. He will pay for this. I will make sure of that.

Tatum is being taken in to the room to get stitches and I am asked to wait in the waiting area until she is finished. I want to be with her, to comfort her but I know that neither of us can help hospital regulations. I sit and wait. I am fuming over the fact that I paid this man to be gentle with her and to strictly just scare her and now my sweet Tatum is in the hospital. I know I got what I wanted out of this, she is mine. That does not defuse my anger. In taking these drastic measures to get her back into my arms, I hurt her. That was never part of the plan.

The nurse came to get me as soon as Tatum's stitches were finished. I walk into her room and sit on the edge of her bed.

"How are you feeling?" I asked her.

"I am a bit tired and the police are going to be by soon to have me speak to a sketch artist. Would you mind standing guard and watching over me until they get here? I need to shut my eyes." She said so quietly.

"Of course." I said, kissing her forehead.

I turn the lights off except for the one by the door and watch her as she falls asleep. She seems alright considering everything she just went through. That's my girl. I knew my plan wouldn't damage her like it would any other woman. Tatum is a fighter. She fears nothing, but our fate I suppose. I fixed that, though. She is now convinced she can stay alive and love me. Tonight could not have played out any better, yes she got hurt and I am absolutely not happy about it. Although it did end up bringing us closer together.

She only got to sleep for a couple of hours before the detectives and sketch artist arrive. I gave them all some space and walked outside for some fresh air. It is about two in the morning and I am exhausted. I am going to find out when I can take her home. I walk over to the nurse's station and ask Tatum's nurse when they are planning to discharge her. Thankfully, that should be happening in a few hours. I will take Tatum back to my place so she can rest without fear. I have to work today but I will make sure she is comfortable and content before I go. I think I am going to try to get off early for her as well. She needs me right now. I'm sure my boss will understand that.

I watch as the detectives leave and the sketch artist isn't far behind. I walk back into to her room to let her know what the nurse told me and see how the interview went.

"The nurse said you can leave in a few hours. I was thinking maybe you should come back to my place this morning so you aren't alone. At least until they catch whoever did this to you." I said.

"That sounds great, thank you for being so sweet." She said, followed by a huge yawn.

"When we get back to my place this morning I will close all the curtains and you can sleep in my bed. I have to go to work for a bit but I won't be gone too long. You can sleep the day away." I told her.

She smiled and motioned me over to her. She pulled me into the hospital bed with her and had me hold her above where her stitches were. This was everything I wanted, I am wrapped up in her and I am her protector. She feels safe with me.

"I love you." She whispered almost asleep.

I kissed her cheek and told her I loved her too. She needed to rest as much as possible. She is also on pain medication so she can't fight staying awake even if she wanted to. I ask the nurse's to be quiet when they come in to check on her to make sure she can stay asleep. They all smile and nod. I just want to take care of her.

A few hours have gone by and I drifted off with her. The doctor comes in and wakes us both, he goes over her list of medicines and how to properly take care of her wound. Once she signs everything we can grab her clothes and get her ready to go. I noticed her shirt was cut and bloody from the attack. Before she could see it I threw it out and gave her my hoodie to put on instead. She looked comfortable. That is all that matters to me. I am warm enough in long sleeves.

"Are you ready to head out?" I asked, taking her hand.

All she did was shake her head yes. I knew she was exhausted and she was just ready to go to bed. I called us a car and helped her step in. I got in next to her and she immediately laid her head down on my shoulder. If I knew how to carry her in without hurting her I wouldn't even wake her to go inside. The poor thing is just so out of it.

We have made it back to my house and I get her out of the car. We thank the driver and I got her inside. I helped her into bed and she cuddled up into my comforter and was once again, asleep. I only had an hour before I needed to go to work, I could lay down with her but I also need to shower. I have only slept a couple of hours and I know I look tired. I don't want to show up to work looking like a zombie.

I decide to just get ready for work quietly and leave her to rest in peace. No more interruptions. I will be back to her shortly. I leave her a note on the bedside table and head on out. She will be here when I return.

Number 15.

Tatum

I wake up and roll over to check the time. It is one o'clock in the afternoon. That is of no surprise after the night I had, Rhys left me a note telling me he would be off by four. I don't really want to get out of his bed. His smell is comforting to me. I feel safe and warm. Which is something I need right now. I am just going to lay here for a bit. There is not rush to be anywhere else.

I look at my phone, it has been blown up with sympathy messages from my boss, co-workers, my friends and family. I don't feel like answering everyone right now but it is comforting to know they all care so much. Last night was terrifying. It wasn't an incident I was not expecting. I guess that's what Olivia was trying to warn me about. She knew something was off. She is like the angel on my shoulder.

I don't know what emotions I am feeling. I am angry and sad, I am anxious and violated, and I am also feeling grateful. I can let my heart want Rhys now. I don't have to fight it anymore. He has shown me that he was right all along. He would save me, he wouldn't put my life at risk like all of the other times before. We really are different people now. We carry the mistakes and heartache from every life but we get to choose what we do and how we handle this one.

I only have a couple of hours before Rhys gets off of work. I should do something nice for when he gets home, to show how much I appreciate him. I could make him dinner, or order in again. I'm not sure how he would feel about me tiding up the place. That may be over stepping his boundaries. I don't have a lot of ideas sense I can't really leave and make it all the way back in time. Maybe I am overthinking this. He wouldn't want me to go all out over him saving my life. He did that because he is a good person. I have a better idea. I will light some candles and we can pick up where we left off. I am not supposed to really be doing any physical activity but if we are slow and gentle I don't see what the harm is. As long as we don't rub against my stitches everything should be just fine.

I loved the idea until I realize I don't even have any cute clothes to put on let alone a nice bra and panties. If I message Rhys and ask him to run by my place to get those things he may assume what I want to do. That would ruin the surprise of it all. I could simply ask him to get me new clothes, ask for a tee shirt and leggings, some clean underwear and a bra. He can choose then and think it is just because I genuinely have nothing to wear.

I pick up my phone and send him the message. The spare key should still be underneath the plant outside. I am usually not one to leave a spare outside of my door like that but this plant is so heavy no one would think to move it. I hope he doesn't mind going by my place. If nothing else it will be nice to shower and put on my own clothes. I am putting on a brave face but I feel disgusting. I know once I am back at home in the quiet with only my mind as company it is going to hit me hard. Especially if they don't catch the man who did this to me.

I don't want to let this ruin me. I don't want to end up so hindered by this trauma that I end up in a headspace like Olivia was. I am going to make a promise to myself, if I start to fall into a deep depression or end up with post-traumatic stress, I will go to a therapist. I will seek help. I won't allow myself to slip too far. I should write this down. I need to find some paper and a pen, if I write it down and put it somewhere at home where I see it regularly then I am holding myself accountable.

I think I remember there being a desk off to the side of his living room. I bet there is something I can use in there. Even if it is just a sticky note for me to hang on the fridge with a magnet. This task means getting out of bed. I need to do this though, it is the only way I will make myself get help if I need it. That subtle, written reminder will be the thing that forces me to do the right thing, should I need to.

Shit. I didn't think about how much a task like walking down the stairs would hurt. Maybe sex tonight is not a good idea. Slow and gentle won't help me escape this fresh wound feeling. I make it to the bottom of the steps and allow myself a second to breathe. I underestimated the searing pain that would accompany a knife wound. The thought of how much of a scar I am going to have saddens me. I don't want a physical reminder of this. How does one heal mentally when there is a memento etched in your skin for the rest of your life? I feel defeated. Now more than ever I need to write this note to myself. I know this ordeal is fresh and I am acting appropriately to it, but to be safe I need to make sure I write this down.

I walk slowly over to his desk and sit down. There is a dark black vase full of pens so there is no searching for that. He has a stack of papers off to the side of his computer but I highly doubt there is something unused to write on. I find a notebook with empty pages, I will just rip one out of here and use it. I turn too quickly and am in such an immense amount of pain that I accidently knock almost everything off of his desk on to the floor. That is just lovely. I now have to figure out a way to pick all of this paper up without putting myself in even more pain. I start gathering each paper one at a time and take it as slow as I possibly can. I can hardly bend without this shooting, ripping pain descending down my entire body. I finally have them all back on the desk, I start to organize them back into the little pile they fell from when I notice something so out of the ordinary that I can't tell if I am hallucinating from the pain I am in.

Rhys has a copy of my work schedule. I don't think there is even a way to make sense of this. No explanation. He absolutely should not have a copy of this. My boss would absolutely not have given him information on when I was working and when I was not. How would he have even come to obtain it?

It hit me like an explosion. The realization on who I was dealing with. I fell for a psychopath. He has been stalking me sense the first day we crossed paths, hasn't he? Everything started to piece itself together. It wasn't fate that threw us into one another, he curated the entire thing. He made me believe that the stars insisted on our interaction. He has been strategically planning every step, every conversation. He manipulated me. He did is so smoothly, I never could have seen this coming. He is the Casanova. I put my trust in him, handed him my heart and was moments away from setting it at his feet. I am unable to move. I should be throwing his shit everywhere and running. My reaction instead is to sit very still. I am going to confront him. I am going to lay out every piece of evidence so that it is not an accusation being thrown at him, but the truth of it all.

I was hit with a second wave of his deceit.

On the schedule sitting in front of me, was something so chilling, I lose my breath. The oxygen in my lungs feels like it has left with the wind that was knocked out of my body. Rhys has circled yesterday's date, with the time I got off. It had information on my closing routine written underneath and a man's name beside it. He hired that stranger to hurt me. To use my blood and my fear to claim me, body and soul. He scared me into giving my volition. I had given him the name hero and fell into his bed. When all I was really doing was loving my attacker of the second degree. I am fueled with absolute panic. How could he do this to me? He put me in the way of death to save me from it.

Did he even know the man he asked to do this to me? I doubt it. Making this so much worse, as if that is really possible. I don't even know if it is safe to confront him with this. Rhys went for master manipulator and stalker to holding hands with my assailant. I don't even have tears left to grieve this betrayal. I am just full of rage. My body is shaking uncontrollably and my soul is on fire in the worst way.

He will be home any minute. I don't have the time to make a practical decision. My only option is to channel Olivia. She is my anchor to strength. With that, I will quickly formulate a plan. One he will not see coming, two can play this game.

Rhys, you have met your match. I will show you what meeting fate looks like.

Number 16.

Rhys

Today has been exhausting. I am beyond ready to walk through my front door and be back in Tatum's company. I have missed her. I am sure she hasn't been feeling great today considering last night's ordeal. She sent me a few messages, but none containing the words I love you. I will have to see what that is all about shortly. I went by her place and grabbed her some comfortable clothes and the flowers I bought her, that were miraculously still alive after over a week of sitting in little to no water.

I didn't think through grabbing the flowers because they are blowing away in the wind off of my bike. I don't think she will mind. I will buy her new flowers tomorrow if she would like. I consider picking up some takeout for dinner but I want to let her choose what we order this evening. She deserves whatever she desires after taking a knife to the stomach. I am still planning on hunting that man down after actually inflicting damage when I explicitly told him not to.

I am finally back in my driveway. The lights are on inside so she must be awake. I hope she slept enough today. I step inside and something in the air just feels off. I see Tatum sitting on the couch. I don't want to startle her, so I start talking to let her know I am home.

"I'm home pretty lady." I say to her.

"Oh hi! I am glad you are back." She answered.

I was happy to hear it. I like knowing she misses me too.

"Did you have a nice, quiet day?" I asked.

"I did actually. I have been in a bit of pain. I accidently knocked over some of your things earlier and hurt myself picking them up." She said.

"Tatum you should have just left it for me to take care of." I said to her, she doesn't need to be hurting herself to clean up something I can easily do for her.

"I know, but there were papers everywhere and I couldn't leave it scattered all over the place." She said, almost cold.

Papers? I don't know what she is referring to. Where in my living room are there stacks of paper she could have knocked on the floor? I start looking around for clues as to what she is talking about.

Fuck. The computer desk.

"Oh. I understand. Thank you for putting them all back in a pile." I said, walking over to the desk while keeping my eyes locked on her.

"Absolutely." She said back, her eyes not leaving mine.

I didn't need to see what was sitting on top of the pile to know what has happened. Tatum knows. She found the copy of her schedule. I was not prepared for this. I executed every detail of this plan perfectly and somehow forgot to shred this last piece of evidence against me. I turn around slowly and she is still locked in on me.

"I can explain, you have to hear me out." I plead.

"Oh I am all ears. You give it your best shot." She said.

"I did this all for us. From the moment I saw you leaving that book store I knew I had to know you. I knew then it was more than an infatuation. We both know that, we are supposed to be together. We don't have a say in the matter. You just kept fighting it and pushing yourself away from me. I had to do something. I never wanted to hurt you. I am going to punish him for that, when I hired him he was told to not physically harm you. It was meant to scare you into believing you would be safe with me. You are, Tatum. You are safe with me. I promise. Just stop denying what is there." I am letting the words pour out of me.

Her eyes are like ice, she has no interest in what I have to say. She had already made up her mind. She believes I am some sort of monster. There is not a single thing I can say to her now to convince her otherwise. I am so angry. How dare she go through my things, she shouldn't have even been over at my desk. She was meant to stay in bed resting until I got home. If she had just listened to me none of this would be happening.

"You think that you're right in this don't you? You believe everything you have done was done out of love?" Tatum asked.

"Yes! It was! You have to see that." I said, walking to kneel down in front of her.

She looked at me dead in the eyes and said something that sparked such vexation I swear I could kill her.

"You are nothing but a sociopath who used the word fate as a way to fixate on a woman who never really loved you." She said, the words seething from her lips like poison to my ears.

I stood up, not losing eye contact and lifted her in the air. She cannot fight back in her injured state. I sit her down on the ground by the corner of the fireplace. I walk away from her and grab rope. Nothing else I have done for her is working. She can't see how much I love her and the lengths I would go to keep her. I will not let her leave this time.

"You see, Tatum. The thing is, there is no way for you to walk away from the fate that was designed for us. You belong to me, whether you like it or not" I said.

She is finally quiet. It is because she knows I am right. She can fight it all she would like, but in her heart no matter how far down it may go, she knows she can't escape who we are.

Number 17.

Tatum

I knew confronting him with his truth was going to unravel events I could not physically with stand. Rhys is evil. I felt it deep down but chose to care for him anyway. I have come face to face with the devil himself. Of all the lives we have lived together, he has now taken form of the thing we owe our debt to.

The way I see it, I have two options. I lay down and take this, I end up dying and fighting this horrid battle all over again in another lifetime. Or I take the ever growing strength inside of me and fight. I am already at a disadvantage sense Rhys took it upon himself to hire a man to brutalize me. Ripping open stitches may hurt, but I will get the chance to live to see tomorrow if I fight like hell. I haven't made it this far to cower down now. I refuse to be the woman who just took the beating. If I die tonight, it will not be because he won. It will be because I took him down with me.

"Tatum, why are you putting up such a fight? You have loved me sense time began." Rhys said.

"What you don't seem to realize is, wherever our souls went in between this life and the last, altered you into someone no person could ever love." I said back.

His face turned red and he balled up his fists. I took a huge breath in and stood up to meet him. The adrenaline moving through my body was a lot stronger than the pain I felt in my stomach. It was almost beginning to disappear. I was ready for whatever came next. I was going to stand against him, no matter the cost.

"Rhys, I don't love you. I don't believe you love me either. I don't even think we were actually created for one another. I think we fell in love our first time around and our lives just stayed tied together. I was never denying that we had a connection, but what you are doing is not okay." I yelled.

Nothing I say will calm him down at this point. This idea of fate has been misconstrued into his way of justifying every horrifying thing he has done to me. In his mind, stalking me, manipulating me and having me attacked was all out of love. His eyes are so dark, so full of hatred.

"You toyed with my head Tatum. You made me believe that you loved me. You are nothing but a filthy liar. I was willing to give you everything. I can tell you one thing for certain, us meeting is going to be the reason you meet your maker." Rhys screamed.

I didn't know fear like this. Last night was a minor glimpse into terror compared to this moment right here. He was going to kill. He wanted to take my life. All because I chose not to love him, because I found out his secrets. There was no manipulating him into thinking I could care for him. I was far too honest in my anger.

I need to run. To really take off and bolt this time. I scan the room for a way to escape. He is standing so close to me, I don't think I can make it around him. Not with a gaping wound on my stomach. I already popped a few stitches in my attempt to get off of the ground on my own. I am at a loss. All I can do is try. I look quickly in one direction hoping he follow my eyes and turn his attention that way so I can get around him. He looks away from me but before I can take two steps away, his hands are around my throat. He shoves me down onto the floor. I can feel each bone in his hand crushing my windpipe. Words cannot find a way out of my mouth. I can feel my fingers trying to break his grip but I don't not think I am consciously aware that it is doing absolutely nothing. I am in fight or flight mode, more fight in this second. My vision is blurring and I feel incoherent. I can't die in this way. Not underneath him. I know I am about to lose, my head begins to turn to the side as my eyes start to close. That's when I notice it, the fire poker. If I can get my hands to it, I can free myself.

I reach with all my might. He is too focused in on me to notice anything else around him. I can feel it. I am almost there. My hands are dripping in sweat, I need to get a better grip to be able to force it upward into him. He shifted his body just enough for me to move my legs up into his groin. He grunts in pain and rolls off of me. I don't have my wits about me very well, but I have enough to know that it is his turn alone to pay this fucking debt.

I crawl the small distance to the fireplace and pick up my weapon of choice. I get onto my knees and I look him right in the eyes.

"You didn't beat me and you sure as hell don't get to beat fate. There is no satisfaction for you this time. It is time for you to get dragged back to hell where you came from." I am screaming at the top of my lungs, tears streaming down my face.

I don't allow him final words. I thrust the fire poker into his chest with every ounce of strength I have left inside of me. I watch as his body jumps forward and his face goes blank. I remove the fire poker from him and plunge it through his body one more time for good measure. I brought the lamb to the slaughter. The devil has his corpse. I am free.

I fall backwards and feel his blood seeping through my shirt. I slide his phone out of his pocket and dial 911. I have no feasible way to process this. The last few weeks of my life have been a storm of catastrophic proportions. I am going numb. I don't want to feel anything anymore.

I hear sirens approaching in the distance. I do not move though. This is where they will find me. Hanging on to the last bit of sanity I have left. I am shattered, broken so extensively I don't see myself ever being whole again. Rhys may not have taken my life, but he took my innocent, simple view of the world and tainted it.

I am no longer human. I am a shell of the woman I once was.

Number 18.

Tatum, Two Years Later.

I am whole again. I left Boston behind. I left everything behind. I got to have a fresh start. I used my traumatic experiences two years ago and wrote about it. I left my heart in those pages and my sadness. I submitted them with an application for a journalist position in New York City. I just recently got the call telling me they would love to have me. I packed a bag that night and I left.

I stayed in a hotel for a few nights and explored my new home. I found a small apartment in the middle of the city and moved in immediately. I have reinvented who I thought I was and became who I was always meant to be. I am proud of myself and all of the things I have done to heal. It took me longer than I would like to admit, but I did it. I am so, unapologetically alive. I take no prisoners and I make every decision based on what is going to make me the happiest. Rhys showed me that life is too short for me to allow other people to have any say in how I live my life. I have become authentic and brave and fierce.

This version of me is everything I wish I had found before Rhys. Things would have been different if he encountered this woman. That is okay though. I have put him behind me.

At times when I see my reflection, I see Olivia staring back at me. I know that she is proud. I did all of this for her, for us. This life threw me the hardest battle I could have ever depicted for myself, but I overcame it. I am better for it. In a way, I am thankful. I have lived. Really and truly lived sense my life exploded from colliding with Rhys.

Things out in the city are just so beautiful. The smells aren't of lemongrass and lavender like back in Boston, more like smells of ambition and hunger. Even the light is different here. The energy is full of power, people dream wildly here. It is infectious. This is why I did what I did. This place is why I fought so hard.

Rhys may not be remembered but I will be. What a beautiful way to be remembered, too. The girl who cheated death. I saved my own life, I was my hero. I embraced the lives I had lost for hundreds of years, looked my mortality in the face and said fuck you.

I broke the ties that bound me to my execution. I no longer owe the stars a debt. I escaped the sick, twisted game the universe had created for me. I did not love him in the end. In his death I find solace. The rope that was stitched around both of our wrists has been burned. He can finally rest now. I do know we loved each other somewhere in time, so I do hope he is peacefully drifting wherever he may be. That he is not angry with me but thankful. We never have to do this life over ever again. Our souls are infinitely freed of one another.

I have a date in less than an hour. I met him on a dating app of all places. I wasn't ready to just bump into someone after Rhys. This guy does seem like the whole package. The man I have been looking for all along. We are finally meeting tonight. At a coffee shop of all places. It has the sweetest little name and it is right in the middle of SoHo. It is called "The Bean".

I throw on a black velvet dress and some of my favorite new gold jewelry. Grab platform boots and a long coat. My hair is wild and I am finally ready. As I approach the coffee shop, I start to get this awful feeling in the pit of my stomach. I know I am afraid because of what happened to me. This feeling should scare me off. Instead I convince myself that I need to go for it.

After all of this time, I really want to get back out there. To find the kind of love I should be given. I put my hand on the door knob of "The Bean" and open it. As soon as I step inside, my heart shatters onto the floor. My eyes met his immediately. I could not breathe. Not a single word could be muttered from my lips. He smiled at me and said-

"I told you I would see you soon."

The End.

Made in the USA
Monee, IL
06 January 2021